Ropes & Reins

Christine Steendam

This is a fictional work. The names, characters, incidents, places, and locations are solely the concepts and products of the author's imagination or are used to create a fictitious story and should not be construed as real.

ISBN 978-0-9939259-6-2

Published by HAZELRIDGE PRESS

PO Box 21 Group 37 RR3
Dugald, MB R0E 0K0

www.hazelridgpress.com

Text set in Garamond; Print Edition

Cover art by VIOLA ESTRELLA
Author photo by MELANIE REIMER

Praise for *Unforgiving Plains*

This is a great book! Get your pajamas on, grab your favorite blanket, get a diet coke and curl up in your favorite chair and enjoy this sweet book.
-Stephanie Lasley, from The Kindle Book Review

It is a great book to curl up with on a cold night with a cup of cocoa to escape into a beautifully portrayed landscape with characters that you will root for…or possibly, thump on the forehead.
— CaSondra Poulson author of *Calling Me Home*

Romance and building suspense come together to make Unforgiving Plains a very enjoyable contemporary western. Ms. Steendam has a writing style that is easy to read. I would recommend this book to readers of romantic suspense and contemporary westerns.
–Denise Moncrief author of *Crisis of Identity*

Christine Steendam is clearly a very versatile writer and the shift from historical to contemporary romance was done effortlessly. I would certainly like to read more contemporary romances from this author.
-Lisa J Hobman bestselling author of *The Girl Before Eve*

There is a depth and richness to each character that makes them come alive on the page. I am keeping my fingers crossed for at least two more books. Please!
— Patricia Grimaud

This is tale worth reading, as readers enjoy the push and pull of opposites against the beauty of the great white north!
— Ind'tale Magazine

Praise for *Heart Like an Ocean*

From page one, Christine Steendam had me hooked and caring about what happened to Senona, a character that I could identify with even though we are separated by centuries. Christine does an awesome job of showing how human emotion and desire flows as one across the expanse of time ... and oceans. I don't want to give any spoilers, but rest assured that you'll feel the roll of every tide right along with Senona and the ending is not one that you'll be able to guess! Can't wait for more from this awesome author!

– Sara Barnard Bestselling author of *An Everlasting Heart* series.

The romance is fraught with conflicts which made me want to tear my hair out at times or melt when the passions ignited.

I rate Heart Like an Ocean 5/5 stars. Recommended for readers who love historical epic tales with a rich cultural backdrop and a mature romance that will tug at your heart strings.

Looking forward to reading more from this author and glad I made this purchase

– Anne-Rae Vasquez author of *Doubt: Among Us*

I didn't consider myself a historical romance reader- but this book has proven that I simply didn't give the genre a chance. I'm definitely a fan!

Eloquent and passionate- this book is a must read.

– C. Elizabeth Vescio author of *Uncontrollably Wasted*

I highly recommend this book- it has action, adventure, great characters and, much like it's main character, exceeds the limits of what it's been labelled; this book isn't a good historical romance novel, it is a GREAT BOOK.

– Andrew Lorenz Creator of *Legacy* and *New Guard*.

To Sabrina.
Thank you for sharing the journey to Heartland with me.

CONTENTS

ACKNOWLEDGMENTS

I always save these acknowledgements as one of the very last things before the book goes to press. I want to make sure I've included everyone who has helped me and brought this book about.

I guess the easiest place to start would be with my publishing team.

Viola, you always do fantastic cover art, but you knocked this one out of the park. Thank you for putting a beautiful face to my work. I swear you must be able to read my mind when you design these covers for me.

Terry, thank you for spending hour upon hour looking over my each and every word. I was nervous to work with a new editor this time around, but you made the experience great.

To my beta readers: Andrew, Heather, Elissa, Jessica, Lisa, and Mom. I can't imagine putting a book out without the valuable input and extra set of eyes you all provide. The story just wouldn't be the same without you.

Thank you to Andrew Lorenz, A.P Fuchs, Melinda Friesen, and Jessica Gollub, my "Writing crew". Thanks for always being just a message away to distract me, unwind, bounce ideas off of, or get opinions from. You guys are a group of writers that are incredibly talented and a powerhouse of publishing information. You're always pushing me to improve my writing and to challenge myself.

Thank you to John and Jana and all the people of Foremost for hosting me on more than one occasion. Thank you for allowing me to experience your town and fall in love with it.

Thank you to Mom, Sabrina, Jasper and Deacon for trekking across Western Canada with me on a whirlwind of a road trip as I wrote this book, gathered inspiration, visited Heartland, and experienced Foremost again. Although that trip was mostly to visit Heartland (the experience of a lifetime!), it is integrally connected with this book in my mind. I've heard it said that a paperback book is a souvenir of the journey the story takes you on. Well, for me, *Ropes & Reins* is the souvenir of that trip.

Thank you to Ellen and Norma, for making possible the road trip that helped spur this book on.

Shaun Johnston, I can't write Tracy's dad anymore without thinking of you. I know, I know, he's not the romantic interest in this book, but I think he has a story coming. And I promise, if it ever becomes a movie, I will insist you're cast.

Thank you to Terry MacLeod for having me on your show, for allowing me to talk about this book as I wrote it. It was my most challenging NaNoWriMo (National Novel Writing Month) yet, and I'm not sure I would have finished those 50,000 words by the 30 day mark if it hadn't been for those weekly check-ins.

Thank you to Kyle. I know I say this every time, but I can't say it enough. Thank you for being supportive, for helping with the kids when I'm crunched for time, for cooking dinner when I'm too exhausted, for understanding when you come home and the house is a disaster because I just "had to finish writing this scene". I know you don't always understand the drive that goes behind writing, but you always, always, always support. Thank you for being my partner in everything.

Thank you to Dad. I think you're probably my biggest fan. For a guy that reads very little fiction, you always read mine, and I really can't express how much that means. I can't wait to hear what you think of this one.

Oh boy, I'm probably missing people. The longer I spend on these acknowledgements, the more people I think of, but eventually I'm going to have to step away and call it done, and I'm running out of space.

Writing may be a lonely profession, but publishing takes a team. So thank you everyone. Whether you performed a job, acted as a support, or just let me know that you were looking forward to the next book, thank you. I really don't know how I'd do this without all of you.

CHAPTER ONE

Slipping her left foot into the stirrup, in one fluid motion Tracy swung her right leg over the saddle, lowering herself onto the seat. She settled into the leather that was molded to her body from all the hours spent there. Her name sounded over the loud speaker, and with barely a touch of her feet, Whiskey Jack moved forward into the alley at an energetic trot.

Coming to a halt, she repositioned herself, shortened her reins, evened them out, and ritually placed the tail of the reins across her left hand.

She breathed deeply, drawing in enough air to fill her lungs to their fullest capacity, and slowly let it out. With the exhaled air, her anxiety and nerves left her body, replaced by the energizing thrill of her thundering heart.

Patting Jack on the shoulder, she braced for the clang of the chute releasing.

Sounds of people in the stands filled her ears, rising and falling in a crescendo around her until that moment, the last second before the steer exploded from the chute. Then, it went completely silent.

Jack tensed beneath her, ready to spring forward. Tracy grasped her rope in her right hand, her reins in her left. She looked over the steer in the chute to her partner and caught

Daryl's eye. She nodded. He nodded back before staring straight ahead.

BANG!

The chute sprang open and Jack hesitated just long enough to give the steer a head start before taking off. Tracy moved as one with her mount, her body seeming to become part of the horse. She deftly spun her rope, expanding the lariat in size with each rotation, and keeping her eyes on the steer running wildly down the arena. Each revolution of her rope seemed as if it were in slow motion, the whirr of it flying through the air just a gentle thrum in her ear. She could hear Daryl loosening his lariat as it flew through the air and caught the steer. She focused on the animal's back legs, and let the rope fly just as the steer kicked up, furious over its capture. The rope slid effortlessly over the legs and the noose pulled tight.

"And it looks like Daryl Higgins and Tracy Miller are bringing the time to beat at five and one. What a run!"

Tracy loosened her lariat to free the steer's legs, and grinned, pumping her fist in the air, her rope gripped tightly in her gloved hand and raised high in triumph.

Daryl took off with the steer toward the out gate, so she turned to follow.

"Hold up, folks. It looks as if Higgins broke the barrier, resulting in a time fault of ten seconds."

Tracy threw up her hands. "Are you kidding me?" Daryl screwed them over at the last three rodeos. He was either too slow or too fast. At this rate, Tracy had no business even considering the Team Roping Finals.

Daryl rode over. "Sorry."

"This is the fourth time! The fourth time, Daryl! You call yourself a professional cowboy? I don't even know how you got enough points to get here."

Tracy dismounted just beyond the out gate.

"Can we talk about this?"

"That's what I'm doing, talking!"

"Tracy, come on! Don't be like that!"

"Sorry, folks, but any domestic disputes must be moved away from the out gate," said the announcer over the loudspeaker.

Tracy stopped and looked up at the booth, a glare blazing in her eyes. She swallowed back a few choice words and clenched her hands into fists to keep from showing the announcer what she really thought of the whole thing.

"Tracy, what's your problem?"

Daryl's hand lighted on her shoulder and she spun around on her heel, her fist flying with the momentum of her movement and connecting solidly on his jaw. His hand flew to his face, cradling his injury.

"What the—?"

Tracy didn't get a chance to hear the rest of what she was sure were expletives exiting her partner's mouth. Two strong hands gripped her arms and dragged her backward.

"That's enough from you," growled one of the men holding her arm in a vise-like grip. It hurt, but she'd never admit that. Anger filled her with a fire that fueled her resistance, even though she knew she'd already lost.

Dragging her through the out gate, the arms eventually let her go, pushing her forward. She tripped to catch her balance, and turned to face them with her hands planted on her hips, ready to take on the next person that came at her.

Daryl walked by, Jack's reins in his hand, and threw them at her as he passed. He didn't even slow down, or look at her, he just kept walking. Bending down, she picked up her horse's reins and walked toward the rodeo grounds.

Her anger simmered as she put Jack in his stall and removed his tack. How could Daryl have broken the barrier, yet again? He knew better. He *was* better than that, and yet he kept doing it over and over. The only reason for it was being sloppy. They were in a losing streak, and she couldn't afford that.

"You're done here," came Daryl's voice from outside her stall.

"You're breaking up with me?"

"It's a bad streak, Tracy. We all have them. But this is ridiculous."

"I can't afford them. I don't have a rich daddy to pay my bills and entry fees."

"Rich daddy or not, you're done. The pro association won't have someone as unstable as you representing them, and even if they let you stick around, no one will ever rope with you again; not after that little show." Daryl strode away, leaving her alone like every other partner she ever had. They all left sooner or later.

She rubbed her fist against her stomach, and choked back a tear. *I won't cry. This is my own fault. I'll get the finals next year.*

She looked down at her right hand and gingerly touched it. It was swelling up already, and a throbbing burn traveled up her arm.

"What were you thinking?"

Tracy closed her eyes and took a deep breath, letting some of the anger cool down, before looking up at the familiar face of Vince Brandon.

"I don't know what came over me," she said, reaching up and taking off her hat. She smoothed out her braided hair with her free hand.

"Will he be filing a complaint with the association?"

"Probably."

"Was it worth it?"

"Nope."

Vince opened the stall door. Sliding in, he walked up and wrapped his arms around her, drawing her into a hug. Tracy wanted to melt. She could fall into his arms and bury herself in his embrace. She always wanted to. But he never felt the same, and now, definitely never would.

After an all-too-brief moment, he took a step back, releasing her. "We should get that hand looked at."

"It's fine."

"It looks broken. If you want to continue roping, you'll have to get that looked after."

"I'm fine," she said through gritted teeth.

"You're not, but you'll figure something out. There's more to do out there than just the rodeo circuit."

Tracy grimaced. Of course, he knew what she was really upset about. Yeah, there was more to life than the rodeo circuit, but she built her whole life around it, and she wasn't ready to leave it yet. Certainly not because she lost her temper. Or because of one stupid mistake.

"Is this your way of making me fight?"

Vince chuckled. "I've never known Tracy Miller to back down from something she truly wanted."

"I backed down from you," she snapped, heat traveling up her face.

"I gave you no other choice," he said, turning around and leaving her alone in the stall.

She collapsed against Jack, and his body heat emanated into her skin. The smell of horse—a sweet mixture of sweat and freshly-cut grass—filled her every sense. It relaxed her more than any drug or bottle of booze could. Horses always were her therapy. She'd grown up on a ranch, and her dad was an all-around-cowboy that got kicked out of the professional circuit after making a run while drunk. He never quite let go of that. But Tracy tried her hardest to make him proud of her becoming a roper.

And now I go and get myself kicked out of the circuit, just like him. Mom was right; I really am my father's daughter.

Stroking her right hand again, she left the stall, struggling a little to close it while using only one hand.

* * *

"It's not broken."

Tracy accepted the news with a huge exhalation of breath, her shoulders slumping with relief. She was fully expecting to hear it was broken by the way it swelled up and bruised.

"What did you do?"

"I punched a guy."

"You must have a pretty mean punch. What does his face look like?" The doctor shook his head as he made a note in her chart.

"Not as bad as my hand. So, what's the prescription?"

"You aren't a patient woman, are you?"

"Do you know many women who are?"

"Good point." He got up and walked toward the curtain that separated Tracy from the rest of the emergency room. "We'll get you fitted with a brace and book a follow-up with your doctor for two weeks from now. Hope you heal quickly, Miss Miller."

"Yeah, me too."

CHAPTER TWO

Tracy rested her right hand on her leg, but couldn't quite relax it due to the brace's hard, unrelenting position. Her left hand gripped the top of her steering wheel as her truck barreled down the highway toward Coaldale, Alberta; home sweet home.

Pulling into the small, five-acre lot she rented and called home, she parked her trailer. It wasn't big. Enough space for three horses in the back—although only Jack currently resided there—and a modest living quarters in the front. It was one of those horse trailer-RV hybrids that were becoming very popular amongst those traveling the circuit.

Tracy hadn't spared any expense on her trailer; after all, it was her home, and still cheaper than a house. Best of all, it was as mobile as she was. Coaldale was her hometown, or had been for as long as she could remember, although in recent years, it felt less welcome. However, her dad lived a few miles away, it was in the heart of Alberta, and she knew people here.

Climbing out of the truck, she walked around to the back of the trailer. "Hey, Whiskey Jack, we're home," she called out, reaching up with one hand to unlatch the bar that held the ramp in place.

Her phone began vibrating. Digging into her pocket, she pulled it out, and flipped it open.

"Hello?"

"Tracy Miller?"

"Speaking."

"This is John Kendal, from the Canadian Professional Rodeo Association."

She closed her eyes and sunk back against the trailer, sliding down until she was sitting.

"What can I do for you, John?" she managed to say in what she hoped was a cheerful voice.

"I really hate to call under the circumstances, but I'm afraid the committee has decided to expel you from the association."

Tracy moved the phone from her face and swore under her breath. Putting it back to her ear, she grimaced and nodded, despite no one being able to see her response.

"How do I get back in?" Silence. "I can get back in, right?"

"If you return to the amateur circuit and earn a thousand points. You've had warnings, Tracy, so we do have to expel you. But if you can prove you're serious, and change your ways—which means, *no* infractions, then I'll approve your application."

"Thanks, John. You'll be hearing from me before the season is over." She hung up before he could respond again, or change his mind, and slipped her phone back into her pocket.

A nicker sounded from inside the trailer, followed by a loud bang caused by the impatient horse's stomping. "Yeah, yeah, I'm coming."

She unloaded Jack and unhitched the trailer, setting her home back up. Once she put everything in its proper place, she grabbed a beer from the fridge and sat down in her lawn chair under the awning that made up her porch. She cracked the beer can open with a hiss and a pop, and brought the can to her lips.

The cold liquid hit her tongue and washed away the bitter taste of disappointment. She couldn't keep her temper in check, and now, she didn't have a clue what to do with her life. How long before it got around town that she was expelled? It didn't take long for news to travel through places as small as Coaldale.

Setting aside her beer, she picked up her phone and entered a ten-digit number. Listening to it ring, she waited for an answer.

"Hello?" The answering voice was gruff and to the point, but oddly comforting to her. Perhaps it was the familiarity that made all her problems melt away.

"Dad, it's Tracy."

"Hey, girly, how was your weekend? Did you place in the money?"

The excitement in his voice only made everything sting a little more. "I would have, if Daryl hadn't broken the barrier again."

"Well, that's the nature of the game. Better luck next time."

"Daryl won't rope with me again."

"Then, find yourself another partner—"

"Dad, I got kicked out," she cut him off.

Silence. She could hear him breathing, but he said nothing. He would, but only when he was ready.

"You'll figure it out. I know you will."

"Thanks, Dad."

More silence. Her dad was a man of few words on most days, and empathizing was not something he excelled at. If she wanted to talk, Tracy had to carry the whole conversation.

"They'll let me back in, if I can get enough points."

"Good. You're going to try for it, right? Get into the Canadian Finals?"

"I'm going to try. The season is already in full swing, and November will be here faster than I'd like. And there's the matter of getting the required number of points ..." she trailed off. It was a nearly impossible feat. She'd have to hit up every amateur rodeo in western Canada to have even half a hope of returning to the pro circuit in time to be eligible for the finals. Not to mention finding a new partner.

"There's always next year."

Those words seemed to define her life; *there's always next year*. There's always next year to settle down, to do even better than before, and to win the top spot in the Canadian Team Roping Finals.

Her phone beeped, letting her know a call was coming in. She pulled the phone away from her face to see who it was, and Vince's name glowed up at her.

"Hey, Dad, I have a call coming in. We'll talk later, okay?"

"Okay."

She clicked off the call and switched to the other line.

"Vince, what's up?"

"Back at home, but not a whole lot. I've been thinking about your situation."

"You're thinking about me? It's about time," she replied, a mischievous crooked smile lighting up her lips, despite no one being there to see it.

She heard Vince sigh on the other end of the line. "Tracy, can you be serious for just a minute?"

"Sorry, it's what I do."

"Look, friends help friends, right?"

Tracy rolled her eyes, listening to him ramble. "Get to the point."

"Right, well, if you need a job, I could use a little help around the ranch."

"And how does your *wife* feel about that?"

"I wouldn't have offered it to you if she wasn't okay with it. The job is yours, if you want it, Rayna-approved and all."

She grinned. Vince was the guy that got away. She met him years ago, here in Coaldale, at a local amateur rodeo. Back when he still did rodeos, that is. At the time, he was dating Jillian, making him unavailable to Tracy. She respected that. Tracy was many things: strong-willed, stubborn, had a short fuse, and liked to get what she wanted. When it came to men, although she wasn't accustomed to losing, Vince was the one guy she never could win. She left him alone when he got married, and he left Coaldale not long after the marriage blew up.

She never got her chance with him. The next time he walked into her life, he'd already fallen in love with Rayna. Now *they* were married, and Tracy was still alone. Not that she cared; she just hated how he kept sneaking into her life.

"I'll be there by the end of the week. Tell Rayna I said thanks."

He chuckled and it sounded warm and inviting. "She cares about you, you know."

"Right, I'll believe that when I see it. I'll see you later, Vince."

She hung up and looked out at Jack grazing in the corral. The setting sun glistened off his golden palomino coat, making him look like part of the sunset.

Setting her phone on silent and putting it aside, she picked up her beer. Something about today had everyone calling her. Maybe that was because it was Monday, or maybe the world just wanted to keep her spinning. Either way, she didn't want to hear the phone ring again today.

* * *

Tracy moved Jack up into a canter as she crested a coulee, riding toward her dad's ranch. He made his home just a short five miles from hers, providing her with a couple hours of riding to get there by horseback. Her sprained, bruised hand rested on her right knee as she grasped her reins in her left hand. She moved with the bounding motion of the horse, the prairie grass passing beneath them in a blur.

Riding up to the ranch, she jumped off Jack, and put him in an empty stall. By the time she left the barn, her dad was walking out of the house to greet her.

"Staying for dinner?" he asked.

"Yep."

"What did you do to your hand?"

"Sprained it."

"Hope the other guy's face looks worse."

She laughed. Of course her dad knew her temper, rather than any mishap, caused the injury.

"His face was pretty hard."

"I can see that. Maybe you should take another swing at him. That brace would help add a little more sting."

Tracy walked into her dad's arms. "Leave it to you to make me smile."

"A father will do anything to see his little girl light up."

He let her go and they walked into the house. Tracy took a seat at the kitchen table and watched her dad putter about.

"Where's Glenda?" she asked, referring to his latest girlfriend. Her mom passed away a few years back from cancer, and now her dad seemed to have a string of lady friends. So far, she hadn't seen any real emotional attachment with any of them. He was just trying to fill an empty space.

"Gone."

"Sorry."

"I'm not. She wasn't your mother."

Tracy laughed. "No one will ever compare to Mom."

"Ain't that the truth?"

They fell into silence. Tracy didn't really know where to go from there. Her mom was a touchy subject. The pain never seemed to fade, and an incessant emptiness filled the air in his home. Getting up, she busied herself by helping her dad prepare dinner. They didn't speak, not even once. Even over dinner, they both stayed quiet.

She started clearing the table while her dad ran some water in the sink. Picking up a dishtowel, she dried as she searched for the words to tell her dad she was leaving town. Sure, Foremost was only an hour away, but she was all he had left. He was why she stayed in Coaldale for this long. That, and she didn't know where else to go.

There really was no nice way to break it to him.

"I'm moving," she blurted out while continuing to rub a dishtowel over a plate with unnecessary vigor, ignoring the fact that it had long been dried.

"Give the plate a rest, Tracy," he said, not looking up. "Where are you going?"

"Foremost, for now, just to tide me over until I can get back on the circuit."

He nodded. "Let me know when you leave. I'll help you load up."

"Friday, I think. But I'm not sure."

Tracy finished drying the last dish, not that there were many with only the two of them, and walked over to the back door. Sitting down on a bench, she pulled on her boots.

"You should come watch me ride amateur."

"You know I don't watch."

Tracy gave him a sad smile. She loved her dad, and they were close, or as close as two independent people could be. They were content to do their own thing, and rarely spent time together, but he was also her first phone call whenever she needed to talk something out. Maybe it was because they could have an entire conversation with only a handful of words being said aloud. But he never came to a single one of her rodeo rides, at least not since he was kicked out of the professional circuit. He watched her in the kid classes, but when he lost his professional cowboy status, he stopped going to the rodeos. It was up to Tracy's mom to take her from then on.

He trained her, though, and spent countless hours teaching her how to rope, and get the timing just right, and the right angle to use so that her smaller stature wouldn't prevent her from roping with the men. He made her into the cowgirl she was today, and she knew he was proud every time she called him to say she won another buckle. She also knew he didn't judge her for getting kicked out. He just didn't attend rodeos. It was too painful for him to see the life he'd thrown away.

She stood up and hugged him. "I love you, Dad," she whispered. She didn't know why she said it, since she hadn't in years. Those three words were some that they never said, but just knew the other felt.

"Love you too, girly."

The acknowledgement brought tears to her eyes and she quickly brushed them away as she pulled back and walked out the door. The screen storm door banged loudly behind her, but she didn't turn around; she just walked straight into the barn and retrieved Jack from his stall.

Tacking him up, she mounted and rode away, careful to avert her eyes from the house. She didn't want her dad to see how much his words impacted her. They shouldn't have. She never doubted her dad's love for her… but something about them being said out loud tore her up inside.

The sun set as she rode home, the sky slowly turning different shades of pink and gold, like an ever-changing painting. The coulees cast long shadows, and as the sun sank lower and lower, the animals of the night started to emerge. Crickets chirped all around and frogs joined in with the bass of their evening song. She rode past a herd of antelope that barely lifted their heads to watch her as she passed by, and quickly lowered them again to continue grazing. They obviously did not see her as any threat.

A truck blew past her on the road, scaring the herd of antelope and kicking up a cloud of dust that engulfed Tracy and Jack. She waved her braced hand around in obvious annoyance, trying to dispel the stifling, gravel dust.

"You live in Alberta and you don't even know how to pass a horse and rider? Moron!" she grumbled.

Red brake lights broke through the cloud of dust before the truck reversed toward her. She pulled Jack to a stop, and waited. *Good. Now I can give you a piece of my mind.*

The tinted window rolled down, and a grinning face greeted her. Immediately, her anger dispelled to minor annoyance.

"Tracy, how's it going?"

"It's going, Shawn. Don't you know better by now than to blow past a horse and rider?"

"Figured that if you're riding the roads, you should be able to keep control of your mount." He winked.

"You're an idiot."

"And you don't look any worse for wear."

"Is there a reason you stopped to talk to me?"

"Yeah, I'm on my way into town. A few of us are going out for drinks. Wanna join us?"

Tracy pressed her lips together and twisted them to one side. *Spend some time with her friends? Or sit at home alone, again?* It wasn't much of a conflict.

"Sure, I'll meet you there."

"Why don't I meet you at your place and give you a ride?"

It was no secret Shawn had been after Tracy for years. They dated briefly, in high school, and occasionally she fell for his cowboy charm after a drink or two. The night would usually end with him kissing her in his pick-up, country cliché and all that, and Tracy always regretted it later on. Every time she did that, she gave him a little bit of hope, although there definitely wasn't any attraction on her part. She considered him a good friend, and nothing more. But if he wanted to give her a ride, he was probably hoping that the night would end the way of a country song.

"No, I'll meet you there."

Shawn tipped his trucker cap and nodded. "Okay, I'll have a cold beer waiting for you."

"That's music to my ears."

Shawn's truck peeled off, leaving another cloud of dust in its wake, and Tracy shook her head, chuckling slightly. She could pretend to be mad all she liked, and if it were anyone else, she probably would have said an earful. But Shawn only did it because he knew it was her, and he liked to get a rise out of her. He was a nice guy, and thoughtful, patient, and considerate. He wouldn't have done that to someone he didn't think could handle it.

Nudging Jack into a canter, she covered the remaining couple of miles home in short order. Going about her evening chores, she tried to swallow her frustration over her less-than-useful right hand. What was Vince thinking? Hiring her as a ranch hand, knowing she would be pretty much useless for another couple weeks? Even getting dressed was a bit of a challenge.

She finally climbed into her truck, pulled her hair into a ponytail, and slipped a baseball cap on her head. Normally, she liked to keep her thick, curly, blond hair contained in a braid, but that was too hard with the brace minimizing her dexterity. Her hat and ponytail would do for now. At least it kept her hair off her neck.

Her truck flew down the gravel roads, covering the distance into town at ninety kilometers an hour, and not slowing down until she hit the paved road that led into town. Pulling up outside the local watering hole, she got out of her truck. She stepped down on the running board and jumped the rest of the way to the ground. Walking in, she glanced around. The bar was full tonight, but there wasn't much else to do in Coaldale on a Tuesday after work.

"Tracy!"

Her eyes went over to the sound of her name being called, and she immediately spotted Shawn waving her over. She smiled and walked toward the table of her friends, grabbing the only empty seat. Of course, it just happened to be next to the guy she was trying not to lead on anymore. Oh well, it wasn't like she chose to sit there. It was the only spot left.

He slid an empty cup in her direction and grabbed the pitcher of golden liquid that sat sweating in the middle of the table, and poured her a glass.

"A beer, as promised."

"Thanks."

The table was full of familiar faces, people she'd known all throughout school until now. Everyone lived in this small town. That's what she loved about Coaldale; everyone knew each other. They'd grown up together, and loved and lost together. It was like one big family. Of course, that came with its downside too.

But one face wasn't so familiar. He sat across from her, his cowboy hat drawn low, hiding his eyes from her gaze and leaving only a strong jaw line visible. Covered in a five o'clock shadow, his full lips were pressed into a straight, uninterested line.

"Hey, stranger," she said, trying to get his attention.

He looked up and a slight upturn at the corner of his lips was as much of a smile as he could offer.

"I'm Tracy," she tried again, extending her hand across the table. "I'd give you my right hand, but it's currently out-of-commission."

That got a raised eyebrow from him as he glanced at the brace, then up at her. Finally, she managed to meet his gaze. His eyes were soft and hesitant, and the way he held himself told her he was uncomfortable. Either he was stuck up, or shy. But the softness in his eyes made her think it was more likely the latter.

He took her hand and gave it a little shake.

"How'd you do that?" he asked, nodding at her right hand.

"Lost my temper."

He raised his eyebrow. Then an arm snaked around her shoulder and interrupted them.

"Tracy is notorious for her flying fists and fast tongue. This girl should have been born a redhead," interjected Shawn.

She swallowed her annoyance. She was actually curious about this newcomer, and the instant Shawn opened his mouth, the stranger seemed to retreat right back into his shell.

"And if you don't watch where you put your hand, you might just be on the receiving end of that hot temper."

Shawn laughed, but his arm lifted off her shoulder.

She remained quiet for a while, drinking her beer and listening to the conversation around her. She kept one eye on the stranger seated across from her, however, waiting for an opening to talk to him again. Over an hour passed, and he didn't say a single word beyond, "Pass the pitcher."

Finally he scraped his chair back and stood up. Tracy watched him. He was tall. Really tall. She wasn't a short woman at five-foot, nine inches, but she was fairly certain that if she stood next to him, she'd only reach his shoulders.

"I'm gonna go grab another pitcher," he said, walking away.

Tracy watched him go. He leaned on the bar, one leg straight, and the other bent at the knee.

Scraping back her chair, she got up.

"Where're you going?" asked Shawn.

"Grabbing a whiskey."

She walked up next to the tall cowboy, trailing her fingers across his back, and causing him to stiffen and tense beneath her touch, before she leaned on the bar next to him. He looked over at her, surprise written on his handsome face and a slight blush crept up beneath his stubble.

"I didn't catch your name earlier."

"Carson."

"What brings you to Coaldale, Carson?" she asked, putting on her most charming smile as she looked up at him.

"Just passing through."

"You don't talk much, do you?"

"I don't find the need to fill the silence with useless chatter."

Tracy frowned. She barely said anything tonight, yet he said the words like an accusation.

"I'm sorry, I didn't realize I annoyed you so much."

His face softened, and he smiled. "I'm sorry, I didn't mean *you*. I just meant in general."

"We don't have to stay here, you know, if you aren't enjoying yourself."

"My ride is here. I'm staying with my cousin, Allen."

"I'll take you home."

Carson raised an eyebrow, but remained silent. It seemed like he was studying her. "Are you trying to pick me up?"

"Would you be upset if I were?"

"I'd think that you're being awfully bold."

"If you don't ask for what you want, you can't expect to get it."

A laugh erupted from him, and not just a little one, but a full-bellied laugh of genuine amusement. She smiled. Most girls might have gotten embarrassed at that point, but not Tracy. She succeeded in surprising him, and she liked that. It gave her the upper hand.

When he stopped laughing, she placed some money on the bar to pay her tab, and turned back to him. "I'm heading out. If you want a ride, feel free to join me. I'm only waiting for five minutes, though."

She walked away, not glancing back. She could feel his gaze burning into her back, and instantly knew she made an impression. She wouldn't have to give him five minutes before he'd be right behind her.

CHAPTER THREE

Tracy reached up to grab the handle of her truck.

"Let me get that."

She stepped down and turned, leaning back against her truck and looking up to meet the brown eyes of Carson.

"Well, that was quick."

"I hate to keep a lady waiting."

Laughter bubbled out of her and she reached up, placing her hand against his chest. "I assure you, I'm no lady."

Carson lowered his head until the brim of his hat touched hers, and his tipped up before falling back and landing on the pavement behind him. They stood, nose-to-nose, breathing each other's air until Tracy reached up, standing on the very tips of her toes to reach his height, and kissed him.

The scratch of his stubble on her chin and the way his lips molded onto hers sent a thrill up her spine. As far as kisses went, this one wasn't bad.

"I think we should go somewhere less… public," he whispered, his lips brushing against hers with every word.

"Yeah, I'd like to get out of this hat."

Another burst of laughter erupted from Carson as his hand planted on the truck beside her. "Do you have a serious bone in your body?"

"Only when you get me angry, then I'm dead serious."

"Remind me not to make you angry."

Tracy scuffed her foot against the pavement and waited for something, anything to move beyond this stalemate of charged emotions in a public parking lot.

"We should go."

Carson nodded and stepped back, grabbing the door latch as he retreated, and pulling it open. "After you."

"Such a gentleman."

She climbed in and he closed the door behind her. She watched him bend over to grab his hat from the ground, but averted her eyes as he stood up. She started the truck, waiting for him to get in the passenger side. A thrill of excitement and nerves rushed through her.

As soon as they were both safely contained in the truck, with only a console separating them, Tracy put the truck into drive and steered it down the main street until she hit the highway.

Silence reigned, broken only by the rumble of the engine. Tracy looked over at Carson, but he stared out his window, drumming his fingers on his knee.

"So, are we going to play this shy, *I-don't-really-talk-to-strangers* game again?"

He chuckled. "Not really sure what to say after that kiss. Words don't really seem necessary."

"It wasn't *that* good of a kiss."

"Speak for yourself."

Tracy glanced over and saw a smirk playing on his lips. It made her want to pull the truck over and kiss him again. Instead, she averted her attention back to the road. Turning up the gravel road that led to her trailer, she hazarded another peek at Carson. He was still staring out the side window. However, he looked bored. And looking bored wasn't good.

Pulling in, Tracy put the truck in park. Carson jumped out the instant the engine turned off and opened her door. She took his offered hand and climbed down. Just as her feet hit the ground, his arm wrapped around her waist and drew her in for another kiss.

She allowed it, but only for a moment before she pushed him back, a playful smile tugging at her lips. "Can we at least get inside before we start making out?"

"There's no audience out here."

"Nope, just Whiskey Jack, but he's the jealous sort."

Carson took her hand and led her over to the trailer.

"I never understood what it was about cowgirls and their geldings."

"I never understood what it was about cowboys and their mares," she retorted.

Carson smiled, and plopped himself down in one of the recliners that took up the cantilever of the trailer. Grabbing a couple of beers from the fridge, she kicked it closed behind her and took the recliner opposite him. Handing him the second beer, she swung the footrest up.

"So, what brings you to town?"

"Rodeo, I guess, would be the short answer."

"Oh?"

"I'm a farm boy, born and raised, but my dad gave me the summer off to try and earn my points for the pro circuit."

"Oh," she repeated.

"You don't sound too thrilled."

"No, that's great for you. What do you ride?"

"Team roping mostly."

Tracy took another sip of her beer. Carson had just gone from an attractive, tall, dark, and handsome stranger, to her biggest competition.

"Just hoping to make it into the pros? Or all the way to the finals?"

"The finals are the dream, of course, but the deal with my dad is the pros *this year*. It's my last chance. If I don't make it this year, my dad refuses to float me through another summer just to pursue a dream. The amateurs don't pay well enough, and if I'm not farming, I'm not making money. As it was, I had to save up and convince my dad I was doing this."

Tracy sipped her beer while she listened. "I know how that goes." Money could quickly become a problem for her too, with her savings woefully low. "Who's your partner?"

"That's why I'm here. Allen, my cousin, said one of his buddies would probably ride with me."

"You should check with Shawn. He was good back in youth rodeo."

Why am I helping him? Shawn was one of the best in youth rodeo. *But not as good as me. And he never went pro.*

"Yeah, that's what Allen said. But I was supposed to talk about it with him tonight, and I took off with the girl he had his eyes on. I can't see him wanting to team up with me now."

Or maybe I'm not going to help him.

"Yeah, that sucks." She tried to make her tone sound disappointed, but even she could hear the hint of glee in her voice.

"You're on the pro circuit, aren't you?"

"How did you know?"

"The mobile living quarters kind of gives it away, not to mention the big buckle you're sporting. That's hard to miss."

Tracy gave him a small smile and took another sip of her beer. "I *was* in the pro circuit; but not anymore."

"How come?"

She lifted her hand and showed off her brace. "My temper got in the way. Look, the finals are something special, and I need to get *all* my points in the next couple of months."

"We could partner. We're both after the same thing."

Tracy grimaced, taking in his hopeful gaze, though he tried to appear nonchalant. "Sorry, but I'm not interested in babysitting a pro-wannabe."

His shoulders seemed to stiffen up and he set his nearly full beer aside. Any charged electricity that filled the air between them wasn't about attraction anymore. Instead, both were steeled up for a fight. Tracy wasn't about to back down from her words, and Carson looked as prideful as she. His jaw tightened, and the brown of his eyes that were, up until now, soft and kind, seemed hard as stone now and just as unforgiving.

"I'm not looking for anyone to *babysit* me. You think I'm here just to find a coattail to ride on?" he ground out through gritted teeth.

She shrugged. "You can't come into the game this late and expect to be competitive."

"I guess I should leave then, before things get more complicated."

"Yeah, you probably should."

"Should I call for a ride?"

Tracy closed her eyes and sighed. Draining the last of her beer, she got up. "I'll drive you."

The drive to Allen's place wasn't long, but given the circumstances, it was a lot longer than she would have liked. The silence made her uncomfortable and tense. With someone like her father, that was okay. With someone like Carson, however, she needed to break the silence in any way possible.

"I guess this is why people either get to know each other first, or don't get personal at all."

"We were well on our way to staying impersonal. You're the one that brought up my reasons for being here."

He sounded bitter, and she let out a snort. "Guess it's my fault you didn't have fun tonight."

"That's not what I meant." It almost sounded like his voice had softened. Regret maybe?

"Good, because it wasn't going to go any further anyway. You can ask Shawn about that."

"Pretty sure I can ask any guy in Coaldale."

Tracy's foot slammed down on the brake, and her truck skidded in the loose gravel, fishtailing across the entire road before jerking to a stop.

"Get out," she said, her voice dead calm.

Carson flung open the truck door and jumped out, slamming it behind him without a word. She watched him walk away as he waved his hand goodbye.

As he disappeared out of the glare of her headlights, she did a quick three-point turn, and flew down the gravel roads back toward her trailer. Tears streamed down her face and she angrily tried to wipe them, only to feel the harsh scrape of the Velcro strap on her brace. She knew she had a reputation in this town, but she always beat it down by ignoring it, and being the best at what she did. Now she was just a disgraced cowgirl, and the easiest girl in town. Even a perfect stranger could see that.

I don't want to be like this. I don't want to be the laughing stock of the town.

Thank goodness she was leaving, but Friday couldn't come fast enough.

Pulling back in beside her trailer, she walked over to the corral and leaned on the fence. It only took a moment for Jack to walk over and nudge her arm, looking for a treat.

"Hey, boy. You don't hate me, do you?"

He nudged her again.

"No, you can't, 'cause I feed you."

She stroked his velvety nose and sniffled. "We're going to a new home, boy. A place where we can be accepted, and start over. You'll like it in Foremost."

CHAPTER FOUR

Tracy loaded Jack onto the trailer and lifted the ramp with both hands, but naturally, her left one took the brunt of the load. She groaned under the weight and put her shoulder into it to get it up the very last bit and clamp it closed. Sighing, she rubbed her hands against her jeans and looked around. Her truck and trailer were hooked up, and everything she owned was stowed away and ready to move.

Jack's corral stood empty, and the rusting metal gate hung open, swaying slightly in the breeze. The water trough was upside down. Once she drove away, there would be few traces that she was ever there.

Maybe her last home held no signs of her, but this town was riddled with them. She didn't go through life being quiet, and kicked up more than a little dust in her years of calling Coaldale her home. People shook their heads when she drove by, and she liked it. She made an impact, and things would be a little quieter as soon as she left.

Climbing into her truck, she rolled down the window and shifted it into drive, slowly moving forward. Once she hit the highway, the wind whipped through the truck and the roar drowned out the music on the radio, leaving her relaxed and eager.

In all her life, she never lived outside of Coaldale, and for the first time, she felt ready to move to a new place; so why not Foremost? It wasn't very different. Just another small town in Alberta with farmers, ranchers, and a main street with everything you required to live, and nothing extra. It was a good life, one that she was used to, just with new people. No one would know her there. Her reputation as an easy woman, or a scorned pro cowgirl would not precede her. She would just be Tracy Miller, ranch hand to Fieldstone Ranch, and amateur rodeo rider with hopes and dreams of competing in the team roping finals.

I just have to find a roping partner.

The drive from Coaldale to Foremost was only a short hour-and-a-half, not much when it came to the Canadian plains. People were used to driving long distances here. When she turned onto Highway 61 West, she clicked the phone icon on her dashboard and waited for the Bluetooth to kick in.

"Call Dad."

"Would you like to call Dan?"

"No! Dan? Really? Do I have a speech impediment? Or are you hard of hearing?"

"I'm sorry, I do not understand your request."

Cursing, she hit the end button and propped herself up on the console with her elbow, trying to get the right angle to dig her phone out of her pocket. On a good day, it would have been a bit of a juggling act, but with only one useful hand, it was practically a circus performance.

The truck swerved across the highway as Tracy triumphantly pulled the phone out of her pocket before grabbing the wheel and steering the truck and trailer back to the correct side of the road.

Resting her brace on the wheel to keep it steady, she dialed her dad's number and dropped the phone on her lap as the Bluetooth directed the ringing through the truck sound system. She placed her good hand back on the wheel and waited for her dad to answer.

"Hello?"

"Hey, Dad."

"Girly."

Tracy smiled at the term of endearment her dad had called her since she was just a little girl. No matter what went on in her life, she could always count on him to make her feel like his special little girl. Problems didn't matter anymore when the simple term "girly" left her dad's mouth because she knew, without a doubt, he would support her in any way she needed or asked him to.

"I'm on my way to Foremost."

"I thought you were going to leave Friday. I planned to help you pack up."

"I didn't have much to pack. Plans changed, Dad. I was anxious to get out."

"Anyone I need to beat the manure out of?"

A giggle escaped her lips. "Manure, eh? Can't even let a cuss word escape your lips?"

"Not in front of a lady."

"I appreciate it, Dad, but you don't have to look out for me, and you don't have to beat the *manure* out of anyone. Vince called me up and said he could use my help sooner rather than later."

The lie escaped her lips as smoothly as if it were the truth. She wasn't so naïve as to think her father hadn't heard about her reputation, but she wasn't about to confirm the rumors, nor would she admit she was running from a life she no longer cared to face. Not now, not after losing the one thing that defined her.

"Well, call me once you're settled. And let me know when you have your first rodeo."

A thrill shot through her. "Are you going to come?"

A sigh sounded over the phone. "No, girly. But I'll be cheering for you from here, and waiting for the phone call to hear about your win."

"What if I don't win?"

"You will. I trained you, and you can out-rope most cowboys I know."

"Thanks, Dad. I'll call you later, okay?"

"Bye, girly."

She reached down and closed the phone, ending the call. She still used a flip phone, considered ancient these days, but it made calls, sent text messages, and could connect to the Bluetooth in her truck, which was all she needed.

Turning up the music, Jason Aldean's "She's Country" piped through the speakers and Tracy lost herself for the remainder of the journey.

Making the turn onto the drive that led to Fieldstone Ranch, her heart began to pound. What if Vince wasn't there? What if Rayna sent her away? It wasn't as if Rayna was her biggest fan to begin with, and now she'd be showing up at their doorstep, unannounced. Leaving for Foremost this morning seemed like a good idea, right up until when she appeared, unexpected, on the doorstep of the one man she always wanted, but could never have.

Despite her apprehension, her foot remained on the gas pedal and her truck crunched over the gravel and up and down coulees as she approached the house. In the past year or so since Tracy was here last, Vince and Rayna had done a lot to turn it around. They repaired the fencing, and cattle could be seen grazing in the front pastures. The sign at the entrance of the drive hung level now, as opposed to hanging from one chain, and had a fresh coat of paint. Potholes that once peppered the drive were all filled and smoothed out.

Pulling into the yard, signs of both care and a woman's touch were evident everywhere at the ranch. The house gleamed fresh and clean white, its red trim still vibrant. Window planters filled with blooming flowers brightened up the house and flowerbeds surrounded the porch. The barn had also received a fresh coat of paint, and now boasted a bright red exterior. It was exactly as Tracy remembered it, yet so different.

Putting the truck into park, she looked up to see the door swing shut and Vince striding toward her. Good, at least it was he and not Rayna. She climbed out, meeting him halfway before wrapping her arms around him in a hug. It was short-lived though, and he put some distance between them before she was ready.

"I thought you weren't coming for a few more days."

"Plans changed. I hope that's okay. I can park my trailer elsewhere for a couple of nights if you need more time to straighten things out," she rambled.

"No, no, it's fine. Rayna will be glad to see you."

"Sure she will."

"There is no animosity here, Tracy. As long as you live in your trailer, and everyone has their own space, things will be just fine."

"That's fine. I like my own space."

"Well, then, I'll let you get settled in. You can park your trailer by the house, or the barn, whichever you prefer, and throw Jack in the back corral. I've got some fencing to repair down the back forty."

"Need help?"

"You just settle in today and make yourself at home. There will be plenty of work for you to start tomorrow."

Vince walked away, leaving Tracy to claim her spot on the ranch. She unloaded Jack first and watched him as he walked into the middle of the dirt corral and lay down, rolling around in the dust and dirt before clambering back to his feet. He shook, starting with his head and the rest of his body following suit, like a wave. The dirt flew off in a cloud as he proceeded to wander around the corral with his nose on the ground, checking out every nook and cranny before settling at the hay feeder and tearing a chunk out. He glanced back at Tracy, chewing in a slow, thoughtful motion that seemed to convey his approval of his new home. Then he returned his attention to the food.

Content that he wasn't going to make a fuss about his new surroundings, Tracy went back to the truck and closed up the trailer. Climbing back inside the cab, she slowly backed the trailer up, positioning it between the barn and the corral Jack was currently standing in. Once she found a good, level spot, she got to work setting up her home. It didn't take long. Tracy lived on the road for two-thirds of the year, and had gotten quite efficient at both packing and setting up her home, despite having only one useful hand.

The last things she took out were her lawn chairs. She unfolded them and climbed up into the trailer, retrieving a beer from the fridge. Taking a seat in one of the chairs and throwing her feet up on the other, Tracy slouched and sighed. She took a long sip of her cool beer. She should probably have eaten something, but the beer seemed so much more appealing after the long drive, and it was already nearing four o'clock.

The thundering roar of gravel being crunched under tires drew Tracy's attention, and she looked over to see an SUV pulling up. Rayna stepped out a moment later, her hair pulled back into a ponytail. She wore jeans and cowboy boots, pulling the whole ensemble together with a more professional-looking blouse and blazer. Tracy almost snorted on her beer. She couldn't believe that Vince actually managed to turn Rayna into a country girl. She went from her shiny, little Audi to a dust-covered Ford Escape, and from skirts and heels to jeans and boots. It was an impressive transformation.

Rayna looked over at Tracy, her hands planted on her hips. Tracy waved and held up a beer as a peace offering. If they had to be living on the same property, she might as well make the best of it.

Rayna walked over and Tracy dropped her feet from the second chair, giving Rayna a place to sit. Accepting the chair, Rayna tipped it up and brushed it off before sitting down.

"Does Vince know you're here?"

"I ran into him before he went out to repair some fences."

Rayna nodded, but looked uncomfortable and unsure.

"Look, you have nothing to worry about with me being here. Your husband has never even looked twice at me."

"Then why does he keep you around?"

Tracy shrugged. "I have no idea. Vince just needs to… help people, you know, that are lost."

"You're the last person I'd consider lost."

"You don't know me very well."

Silence fell between the two women. Tracy could've kicked herself. That was such a great way to start out with Rayna.

"Look, I won't be here very long. I'll be gone to the next rodeo and then I'll only be stopping here when I have downtime." Rayna nodded. "I'm not trying to hone in on your territory, nor am I trying to cause problems between you and Vince. I can pack up and leave right now. Vince won't have to know that you asked me to."

She shook her head. "No, it's fine. I trust Vince, and I should probably trust you. You've never done anything to make me think otherwise."

"Thank you."

"Foremost Rodeo is in a few months. Will you compete?"

Tracy nodded. "Sure will."

* * *

Rays of warm light fell across Tracy's trailer and she stretched, rolling over to look at the time. 6:30 a.m., the alarm clock read. She groaned, pulling the blanket up over her head.

Bang, bang, bang.

"Rise and shine, Tracy!"

"It's not even seven. Go away."

"The beasts need feeding and I'm not paying you to lie in bed."

"This beast needs sleeping."

She heard the latch of her trailer door release, and the whole trailer shifted a bit under Vince's weight as he climbed up the step and poked his head in.

"I come bearing peace offerings," he said, stretching his hand in with a steaming mug of aromatic coffee.

Tracy emerged from under the blanket and slowly sat up. "That does look good. But coffee isn't exactly food."

"By the time we finish with morning chores, breakfast will be ready and waiting. C'mon, get dressed and meet me in the barn."

The mug of coffee stayed behind on the counter as Vince retreated and closed the door behind him. Falling back down, Tracy rolled over and off the bed, landing on her feet. She slowly moved around the trailer, getting dressed and brushing her teeth. Rather than struggling to get her hair into a ponytail with her hand in a brace, she threw on her cowboy hat and tucked her wild curls underneath. She'd have to tame them later, when she had more energy.

Picking up the now lukewarm coffee, she took a gulp and walked outside. The warm summer air greeted her and caressed her skin in a welcomed gesture. She smiled, walking the few steps into the barn. Taking another large gulp of caffeine, she walked over to where Vince stood in a stall.

"Where do you want me, boss?"

"Go throw some grain to the horses in the corrals and check all the troughs."

Tracy drained the last of her coffee and walked into the feed room. Setting the mug on the shelf, she went about filling a pail with a mixture of different pellets and feed before going back outside.

Even though she'd never done chores there, she went about things like it was second nature, running out the hose and starting it to fill one trough while she divvied out the feed, then moving the hose to another trough. There were four good-sized corrals in the yard, one on either side of the barn and two behind it. A small, five-foot walkway ran between each corral in the back. Behind the corrals was pasture, with the gate near Tracy's trailer.

It was a nice setup. When Tracy was here a couple of years ago, there was only one big holding pen and the pasture. There also weren't as many horses. Vince and Rayna must have been doing pretty good for themselves. But, that could have also been thanks to Rayna's real estate company, which she opened in Lethbridge. She specialized in farmland and acreage in the surrounding areas—like Coaldale and Foremost. As far as Tracy could tell, she was making quite the name for herself. She had a good reputation for honesty and shrewd business sense, at least according to the talk Tracy heard around Coaldale.

"Breakfast!" Rayna called from across the yard.

Tracy looked up and waved a greeting to Rayna, who stood on the porch with one hand resting on a rustic wood post. She was leaning against it as she waved back before looking out to the fields.

Tracy finished feeding the horses and turned off the water, neatly stowing away the hose before going into the barn to tell Vince that breakfast was waiting.

"Rayna called," she said, passing by him just as a forkful of shavings and manure flew out and landed in the wheelbarrow that was sitting in the aisle.

"Perfect! I'm starving."

She threw the empty pails in the feed room and grabbed her mug off the shelf.

They walked together across the drive. Tracy let out a chuckle as she noticed their strides moving in sync with each other.

Climbing up the stairs, Vince ran up them two-at-a-time before putting his arm around Rayna's waist, and pulling her to face him in an almost dance-like motion as he planted a kiss on her lips.

"Mornin', beautiful."

She playfully shoved him away, but the way she smiled up at Vince told Tracy that she absolutely adored him. The love they had for each other seemed to radiate off both of them, making it impossible to ignore.

The three walked into the house, but Tracy held back a little in silence, giving Vince and Rayna more space. She kicked off her boots by the back door and grabbed a seat at the kitchen table, which was already set and filled with bacon, eggs, and hash browns.

"This looks delicious, Rayna."

"Thank you. You guys better dig in, I have to get ready for work."

Looking up at the clock, it was only 7:30, but Rayna had an hour-or-so drive ahead of her.

Vince got up and walked with Rayna to the door, leaving Tracy alone in the kitchen. Tracy tried to busy herself so she didn't have to think about the soft whispers of love passing between the husband and wife. It's not like she was upset that it was Vince—having long ago accepted he'd never be hers—she was jealous of how happy and content they seemed. She noticed how even the sight of each other seemed to light up their day. She'd never had that with anyone.

Vince returned a minute later and sat down, heaping his plate full of food.

"More coffee on the counter if you want."

"Thanks," she replied around a mouthful of food.

"So, what's your plan for the next little while?"

Tracy shrugged. "Gonna head out to the Coalhurst rodeo next weekend, be back for work the following Monday."

He nodded, shoving an entire strip of bacon into his mouth.

"I need a roping partner, though. Know of anyone who would be willing?"

He shrugged and swallowed. "I'm sure there is someone. Want me to make some calls?"

"Sure."

"After breakfast, I'll need you to head out and check on the herds in the far pastures. Are you good with that, despite your bummed hand and all? I assume you can handle it if you plan on roping."

"Yeah, that's fine."

"I think I heard maybe Rodney's son wants to break into the pros. I'll go by and see him today."

"I appreciate that, Vince. You didn't have to do all this for me—offering me a way out."

"Hey, don't worry about it. I know what these small towns can be like. They're like one big family when things are going right, but when things go wrong, you're gossip fodder. No one means any harm, but it's hard."

"Still, you didn't have to do this."

"I know, and you would have pulled through just fine without me, but I thought it was time you got out of Coaldale and started living around people you haven't known since you were knee-high and into sheep wrestling."

Tracy snorted. "I was the queen of sheep wrestling!"

"I don't doubt it! You were probably the queen of everything you tried, which makes it all the worse that you lost pro status."

She nodded. Pushing her chair back and picking up her empty plate, she deposited it in the sink. "I'll go check on those herds. See you later."

She didn't wait for Vince's response before walking out. Grabbing her saddle out of the tack room in her trailer, she hesitated and looked at her lariat hanging on the back corner before grabbing it too. She didn't know if she could even rope with the brace on. Out in the pasture, however, no one would see her fail if she couldn't.

She caught Jack, and worked in silence, when normally she would have been chatting away to the horse.

Gripping her rope, she mounted and rode out to check the fence lines. Riding up to a herd of heifers, she unwrapped her rope. She fumbled with the starched lariat, her fingers refusing to cooperate as the stiff brace got in the way. Finally, getting it in the correct position, she swung her arm in an arc. The rope slipped from her fingers, falling into a heap on the ground.

"Crap!"

Her throat and eyes burned as she tried to hold back hot tears of anger. This was a load of manure, as her dad would say. She had to rope. She was the best roper in Eastern Alberta, and she wasn't going to let a stupid sprained and bruised hand change that.

Dismounting, she collected her rope and tied it to the saddle, pinning the rope against the leather with her elbow while using her hands to clumsily tie it in place.

Mounting again, she nudged Jack forward with the side of her foot and rode off at a jog toward the fence line. It took a couple hours to ride all the pasture fence lines, but most of them looked in good order. In the steer pasture, there were a couple of posts leaning a bit, likely from cattle scratching themselves on them. They'd have to come back out later and fix those.

Riding back toward the house, she saw Vince still hadn't returned, so she put Jack away and went into the barn to find something to keep her busy. There was never any lack of work around a ranch; she knew that from growing up on one, you just had to be willing to keep busy. And right now, the last thing she wanted to do was sit around and feel sorry for herself.

CHAPTER FIVE

Carson drove up to his dad's farm. He could see the seeder out in the distance, driving back toward the yard. Leaning against the truck, he waited. Minutes later, the seeder pulled into the yard and stopped near one of the three metal machine sheds. His dad climbed out, moving slowly, as if his joints needed oiling. When his feet hit the ground, his right hand went to the small of his back and he arched it, stretching. He was getting too old to sit in a tractor all day—his arthritis seemed to worsen every year, but the stubborn man refused to hire someone until Carson decided what he wanted to do with his life.

Carson knew he should be the dutiful son and take over the farm, but every time he thought about walking up to his dad and telling him he'd stay, he got a sick feeling in the pit of his stomach. He felt trapped. He always wanted more out of life than just working the land. Growing up, his heroes were cowboys; the guys who could work up the gumption to sit on a wild bronc, and ride out the longest eight seconds of their lives. Guys who spun ropes and caught cattle like the days of the Wild West. Some boys wanted to be Superman, Carson wanted to be a rodeo star. Dreams of the road and arenas don't just fade away. Farming required setting down roots, and he wasn't ready for that. Thirty years of age and he still couldn't bring himself to make a home, find a girl, and have a family.

Maybe something is wrong with me, he thought. *Fear of commitment or something.*

He waved to his dad and heaved himself off the truck into a standing position. He walked over—his dad shouldn't have been moving any more than he had to.

"You're back early. Any luck in Coaldale?"

Carson couldn't contain his grin. "Yep. Got myself a heeler for the Coalhurst rodeo next week." He managed to convince Shawn to rope with him. He refused to promise anything more than Coalhurst, but it was a start.

His dad grunted. "So you're not here long, eh?"

"Just picking up Danny-boy and I'll be on my way again. We have to practice a lot before next weekend."

His dad nodded and clapped his hand on his shoulder. "I'll see you in Coalhurst then."

"You're coming?"

"I've been watching you rope since you were knee-high; I'm not about to stop now," he said in a gruff voice, as if Carson's surprise insulted him.

Carson stared at his father. His eyes hurt, so he knew they were open wide, and he clenched his jaw tightly just to be sure his mouth wasn't hanging open. Normally, his dad would never have taken time off from the farm to watch a rodeo, much less in a different town. The farm always came first. Crops and the weather didn't take time off just because something was going on, so farmers couldn't either. Which was exactly the reason why putting down roots here scared Carson so much. A farm wasn't just a job, or a lifestyle; it was a prison, and the heaviest ball and chain Carson knew.

"I, uh, I'll see you then, I guess," he replied, not really sure how to respond to his dad's sudden interest in his life. His dad kept pushing him for years to make a decision; maybe he was just giving in, and realized that Carson wouldn't be the one to take over the family farm.

A truck pulled in, followed by a cloud of gravel dust; it parked beside Carson's truck. The big, red Dodge wasn't unfamiliar to Carson. Vince Brandon had become a staple around Foremost for the last six years or so.

"Hey, Vince," his dad called out. He waved as Vince climbed out of the truck and walked over.

"Rodney, how's it going?"

"Can't complain. Weather's been good, so life is good."

Vince nodded as if he understood.

"Carson, did I hear you were hoping to break into the pros this summer?"

"Yeah, that's the pipedream. It's a lot of points to make up in a short time, though."

"You do team roping?"

"Sure do."

"Need a heeler?"

Carson smiled. Now people were coming to him? He'd just driven to Coaldale in search of a heeler, because he couldn't find someone here.

"I actually just found one for the Coalhurst rodeo, but he's only committing to that one. I might need a heeler after that."

"That's less than ideal, but I think I can convince her that you're worth letting one rodeo go. This girl I know is one of the best ropers in all of Eastern Alberta. She ran pros, but had a bit of a mishap."

"I don't know. I'm not looking to help someone relive their glory days."

"She's still *in* her glory days, let me tell you! She was a strong contender for the finals if she hadn't gotten kicked out. She'll get you to the pros this summer, if that's what you want."

"That sounds good, eh, Carson?" his dad chirped.

Carson slowly nodded. "This girl wouldn't happen to be Tracy Miller, would she?"

"You know her?" Vince's face seemed to light up.

"Met her, had a disagreement and moved on. I'm sorry, Vince. I can't work with her."

Vince let out a chuckle. "Tracy would make enemies with her best chance at getting back into the pros. Well, good luck in Coalhurst. But I'm telling you, Carson, you might want to reconsider. I know you did well back in the day, but you're also out of practice, and you need a strong heeler to carry you forward. You might take Coalhurst, but once Tracy becomes your competition, you won't be picking up the number of points you need."

"She's got a bummed hand. I don't care if she gets that brace off, her hand will still be weak. I'll take my chances against her."

"Carson," his dad tried to cut in.

"No, Dad, you didn't meet her. Thanks for thinking about me, Vince. I appreciate it, but it just won't work."

He stalked off, leaving Vince and his dad behind. Entering the small barn that was really more a glorified shed than anything else, he grabbed his saddle off the rack. The stock trailer sat parked beside the barn, so he threw it in the front compartment and returned for the rest of his tack and supplies.

Glancing over to where he left Vince and his dad talking, he saw Vince driving away. He waved, and walked over to his truck. His dad was already climbing back into the seeder. Good, he wasn't really interested in talking. Thing is, if he had known Tracy needed a header—someone to rope the steer's head—a couple of days ago, when he'd been at her trailer, he would have gladly accepted. She was the type of woman who didn't have the word "lose" in her vocabulary, and that is exactly the kind of partner he needed. But the minute he revealed he wanted to get to the pros, she saw him as competition rather than as a potential partner; and when he mentioned teaming up, she got downright rude. He couldn't work with someone who was in it on her own. She could be the best roper in all of Alberta, but if she were in it for herself and not for the team, he'd end up back on the farm a lot faster than he'd like.

It wasn't that he didn't like her. Quite the opposite, he was immediately attracted to her. From the moment she walked into the bar with her curly, blond hair tucked up under her cap, he felt drawn to her. Then she walked right over to the table and sat across from him. It was almost like fate was shoving her into his lap, but he was too nervous to even open his mouth until she forced a conversation. After that, she put him at ease and he could open up.

Too bad she was set on doing things for herself, her way, and *only* her way. Vince was the second person to tell him she was a great roper. Allen had already given him an earful over being more diplomatic with the best roper in town. If only he'd known that before he'd gone to her trailer.

Jumping into his truck, he backed it up to the trailer with practiced ease and hooked up the gooseneck.

He whistled, and his horse, Danny-boy, trotted over. He was Carson's pride and joy; a compact, muscled, black quarter horse with four white stockings, and his face was almost completely white. He caught attention wherever he went, and his one blue eye seemed to put fear into the cattle. Carson raised the horse from a colt and trained him on his own. Danny-boy had cows in his blood, and loved nothing more than the chase.

"Hey, boy, you ready to chase some cows?"

The horse tossed his head as if to say *yes*, evoking a chuckle out of Carson. Carson wasn't so great with people, but this horse could communicate with him as if they both spoke the same language.

"Yeah, me too. Enough of this farm life for us, eh?"

Danny-boy lowered his head and touched Carson's arm with his nose. Yep, this expressive horse understood him better than anyone else. He knew his horse wanted to rodeo as badly as he did, and he'd give his all to win in that arena next weekend.

CHAPTER SIX

Tracy looked from Vince over to Rayna and then down at her plate of food. The three of them sat around the table, but the air felt heavy with tension from unspoken words. She could tell Rayna wanted to talk to Vince by the way she kept glancing at him, but it seemed she didn't feel comfortable enough to talk about her life in front of Tracy.

"So, I spoke to Rodney and his son today. Seems Carson already has a heeler."

Tracy halted, her hand hanging halfway to her mouth with a forkful of food. "Carson? He's from here?"

Vince had a sparkle in his eye that spoke of mischief. "So you know him?"

"From the look on your face, I'll venture a guess that you already knew that."

"He didn't seem to take too kindly to your name being mentioned."

She shrugged. "He deserved it."

"You can't estrange everyone you know if you want to go forward in life. You need a roping partner, and so does he. It would have been the perfect fit, and yet you ran your loud mouth and ruined that."

"I'll find a header on my own, thank you very much. And he's not a perfect fit. He's an untested *nobody*. Perfect is not babysitting."

She pushed back her chair, leaving the table without another word. Allowing the door to close with a slam behind her, just to reinforce her annoyance over Vince's meddling, she collapsed onto the porch step and sighed. Dropping her head into her hands, she let the calm of the evening air wash over her. A few deep breaths and she'd be okay. Her mother taught her that. She got her quick temper from her dad, though you'd never guess that now. Her mom had a lot to do with how her dad was now too, the mellower, more laid-back version of him.

Tears burned her eyes. *Mom, I really need you right now,* she thought, grinding the palms of her hands into her eyes to stop the tears before they could really get started. She knew if she let them flow, she wouldn't be able to stop them. The last thing she needed was for Vince to walk in on her, a girly, crying mess. She worked hard to portray herself as strong and unemotional as the guys she rode with. She had to. There weren't many women in team roping—of course, since she'd been kicked out, now there was one less.

"She's a grown woman! She doesn't need your interference," Rayna's raised voice carried through the open kitchen window, drawing Tracy's attention. Rayna's tone of voice told Tracy their conversation was already well into the depth of the problem.

"She's a friend."

"I know, which is why I said you could help her out. But this getting involved, and telling her how to live her life, and trying to fix her…"

"Rayna, you have no reason to be jealous."

"I'm not!"

Her words sounded defensive. Like this wasn't the first conversation they had about her, or about Rayna's apparent jealousy. Not that Tracy blamed her. She would have been jealous if she were in Rayna's place.

"You let me spend time with my daughter and Jill, and get involved in their lives, but Tracy isn't okay?"

"That's different and you know it. You need to leave her be, Vince. She is not *your* problem. If she wants to screw up her life, let her."

"If people went through life with that attitude, I'd probably be rotting in a prison cell right now…"

Tracy got up and walked away, letting the raised voices drift off in the distance. She didn't want to hear a marital fight caused by her. As much as she liked Vince, she couldn't and wouldn't be the source of any problems between Rayna and him.

She walked out to the corral where Jack quietly grazed on some hay. Slipping between the two fence rails, she climbed in and walked over, resting her head against his neck and breathing in the sweet grass scent of her horse.

"I think I'm screwing things up again," she whispered into his neck.

No response. Of course. She was talking to a horse, and even though Jack had an uncanny ability to respond in an almost human way, he seemed uninterested tonight.

"Where do we go from here?"

Jack swung his head around and nudged her.

"Yeah, nowhere. No one wants us. It's time to move on, boy."

She gave Jack one last pat, then walked back to the house. She could see Vince sitting outside on the step with Rayna, sipping coffee. All looked to be well in paradise again, all forgiven and forgotten. She watched Rayna sit next to her husband and lean against him. He sat one step higher than she, and his legs provided a solid wall for her to rest on. As Tracy approached, she heard hushed words floating through the evening air before a quiet laugh came from Rayna.

Rayna looked her way and fell silent, but the forced smile that stretched her lips let Tracy know her decision to leave was the right one. Vince and Rayna didn't need her getting between them.

Tracy didn't sit. She just planted her boot on the bottom step and held onto the post.

"I'm going to get right to the point. I appreciate your willingness to take me in and help me out with my life, but I'm not your responsibility, and I'm not ready for settling down to a ranch life. I'm a nomad; always have been." She paused, but never let her gaze waver from Vince and Rayna. "I'll gladly help out for the rest of the week in exchange for letting me park my trailer here. But come next weekend, I'm packing up and heading to Coalhurst. And from now on, I'll be dining alone."

Rayna nodded, and the slight upturn of her lips looked genuine this time, like she was saying *thank you*.

"Are you sure?" asked Vince.

He flinched as Rayna's elbow connected with his knee.

Tracy smiled, feeling more confident in this decision than she had in any of her recent ones. "Yes, I'm sure."

"Okay. But you know where we are if you ever need a place to park your trailer."

"I appreciate that. And I might just take you up on it from time to time. But if all goes according to plan, I'll be on the road all summer."

"Winter?"

"I'll cross that bridge when I get there. But I don't think my place is on Fieldstone Ranch."

Tracy let her hand drop off the post and shoved it into the back pocket of her jeans, then turned on the heel of her boot and walked back to her trailer. If felt good to get that out; now her decision was made. Everything about coming here, to Fieldstone Ranch, and to Vince, felt wrong. The weight that lifted off her, and the accompanying sensation of lightness she felt after stating her decision, only made it all the more apparent that this definitely wasn't the place for her.

Collapsing into her worn-out easy chair, she grabbed her cellphone from the side table and flipped it open. No missed calls. No text messages. No one missed her.

She still needed to find a header, though. Scrolling through her contacts, she looked for someone who could help her out. She paused at Shawn's name after the second time of scrolling through her entire list. He might be her only choice at this point.

Pressing the call button, she carefully lifted the phone to her ear and listened to it ring.

"You left town pretty quick," Shawn said, without any hello and sounding uncharacteristically annoyed.

"Sorry, a job came up."

"Cool."

Normally, Shawn was a lot more upbeat. "Are you mad at me?"

"Why would you think that?"

"I don't know," she bit back. "Maybe because you're being short with me."

"I thought we had an understanding, Tracy. You left town without so much as a goodbye, right after you took that Carson home with you."

"Nothing happened."

"I know. Nothing ever happens with you! I know that *all* too well. You play at being some kind of bad girl to hide the fact that you're just scared. You think I can't see through you?"

Tracy sighed, trying to stifle her annoyance. Shawn had no right to be upset with her over that. It wasn't like she *ever* made any indication that something would happen between them. He had no hold on her, no control, and no right. And she definitely wasn't *scared*.

"Look, I didn't call to talk about Carson or my leaving town. I need a header for the Coalhurst rodeo next weekend. Are you in?"

Silence.

"Shawn?"

"I already agreed to partner with Carson."

Tracy took the phone away from her face and cursed under her breath. Bringing the phone back, she put on a smile, knowing that it could be heard through her voice, and started again. "Well, if you want to partner with him, I completely understand. But he's looking for a heeler and we both know your strength lies in being a header."

"I gave my word, Trace. That means something to me."

"I know. Well, good luck. I'll see you there."

"'Night."

Tracy hung up, feeling a little sick. She'd give it a day, maybe two, and her phone would be ringing to see if she still needed his help. He never could turn her down. And she hated taking advantage of that.

CHAPTER SEVEN

Carson sat at the kitchen table in Allen's house. He sipped his coffee and looked out the window at his horse, Danny-boy, grazing in the pasture behind the house.

At least one of us is calm. His knee bounced up and down as he tapped a staccato beat with his foot and took another sip of coffee. He glanced up at the clock. Shawn would be here in an hour to practice.

"It's just some team roping. Settle down," said Allen, walking in the back door.

"This is my last chance at the rodeos. After this, I have to give my dad some kind of decision."

Allen shook his head and sat down opposite him, a steaming mug of coffee enveloped between his hands. Allen was a massive guy, and not in the fat sort of way. He stood as tall as Carson's towering six-foot, three inches, and twice as wide, built like an ox. The man was all muscle, and not someone who should be messed with.

"So stop being so nervous. Either you make it, or you don't."

Carson nodded. His cousin was right, of course. The man was much more laid back than he was. He seemed to be happy with his life, his ranch, and his home. He showed a lot of promise in the rodeo circuit, but left it all to work his dad's ranch.

"Wish you would just rope with me."

Allen shook his head. "Nope. I'm done. I was never much of a roper anyway."

Getting up, Carson carried his mug to the sink and let it clatter into the stainless steel basin. "Yeah, true. I'm going outside to get Danny warmed up. I'll see you later."

He pulled on his boots and let the screen door slam behind him, a victim to gravity and broken hydraulics. He wanted to be ready when Shawn arrived. He couldn't afford to give him any reason to think he wasn't worth it.

By the time Shawn pulled in, Carson had been riding patterns with Danny-boy for over half an hour. He directed Danny toward the fence and trotted over. Coming to a stop, he waved, but all he got was a nod in response. Shawn jumped out of his truck and walked around to the back of his trailer to unload.

Allen had the ideal place to practice. He let Carson pull a few steers from his herd, and even had a chute ready in the riding arena from back in the day when he did steer wrestling. It was unused for a number of years now, but he could still remember when his uncle first set it all up for Allen.

Carson had been standing on the bottom rung of the fence as Allen, his uncle, and a couple of ranch hands wrestled the heavy chute into place. To say Carson was green with envy would have been putting it lightly. He'd always been jealous that his cousin did the minor rodeo stuff all summer long; and the new home setup was only icing on the cake. At least, his dad had let him live there for a couple summers, back when he was too young to be a whole lot of help around the farm. But once he knew how to run the machinery, there were no more rodeos with Allen; just one or two when they weren't busy, and if the venue was within a two-hour drive. That was the life of a farm boy: you earned your keep or you didn't eat. Maybe not quite that harsh, but everyone was expected to pull his own weight.

Shawn walked over, leading his already tacked horse. She was a compact and muscled little quarter horse mare. Opening the gate, he walked in and mounted without saying a single word to Carson.

He watched Shawn ride some patterns, warming up the mare. The guy knew how to ride, he'd give him that much. But riding was only half of what the rodeo business required.

"Ready to get started?"

"Sure."

Shawn sounded less than enthused. But he shook it off and rode over to the chute. As the heeler, Shawn would have to pull the chute, and allow Carson to rope the head first. Once they got to the rodeo grounds on Friday, they could make a few runs together with someone else pulling the pin. Carson didn't expect to come into the money in Coalhurst, but it'd be good practice, and that's what they needed right now. He also needed to convince Shawn to stay on with him.

Shawn lined up his horse next to the cattle chute where a single steer stood, pawing at the sand. He let out the occasional snort, but had been making quite the racket all morning. Carson managed to block it out for the most part, but now that they had to actually work with the animal, even the slightest restlessness put him on edge.

"Ready?"

He nodded, tightening the grip on his rope. The latch pulled with a loud clang and the chute sprang open, allowing the upset steer to exit its confines. It ran as fast as it could for the other end of the arena.

Danny-boy sprang forward the instant the gate opened, and Carson's rope whizzed through the air with a hiss. His horse kept pace with the steer, and he let the rope fly. The loop was beautiful and wide, almost perfect. Time seemed to slow down as the lariat arched through the air and his heart pounded in time with the footfalls of his horse. The lariat began its downward descent. The steer gave a kick, and the rope fell harmlessly to the ground.

"Seriously? That was a near perfect throw!"

Shawn rode up, bringing his horse to a sliding stop beside him. "Perfect throw doesn't mean much if you don't have your timing down."

"Yeah, thanks for that. I know how to rope."

"I'm sure you did, once upon a time. But it's not like riding a bike. It takes time to get the feel back."

Shawn was right, and he knew it. But a small part of him thought, or *hoped*, that maybe he was still as good as he thought he was as a teen. That little bit of a fantasy played over and over in his head: riding into the arena and making the time-to-beat because he was a natural. He knew it was nothing more than overindulgent daydreaming, but that didn't mean he couldn't hope it would happen.

"Let's just run through a few times with just you. You're rusty, that's all."

He nodded, and Shawn squeezed his horse forward to chase after the steer. He watched as Shawn caught the beast with practiced ease and wrapped the rope around his saddle horn. His mare dragged the steer, bucking and fighting, the whole way back to the chute. Once he was back in, Carson lined up and prepared to go again.

And again.

And again.

They went for over an hour. Danny-boy dripped in sweat, Carson's arm ached, and the steer snorted and huffed.

"Enough. You got him once."

"Pretty sure that was fluke," ground out Carson in frustration.

"You'll get it, just gotta keep practicing. But you won't get him again today."

He nodded. "Fine. Tomorrow?"

Shawn shrugged. "I gotta work. But I'll be by after supper."

"Sounds good. Gives me some time to practice during the day."

"Don't be too hard on yourself, man. You can't expect to come from nothing up to pro level in one season."

"I gotta."

"You won't. Just realize that now and you won't be disappointed. Some guys rope for years and never get there."

"I will."

He could tell Shawn didn't believe him by the way his lips pressed firmly together in a straight line. Allen said pretty much the same thing when he first came to him, searching for a roping partner. Maybe that's why his dad offered him this deal—an impossible one for him to win.

"See you tomorrow."

Carson dismounted before walking his horse to the rail. He untacked, going through the motions on auto-pilot, while his mind spun in circles. One voice kept taunting him, telling him he wasn't good enough, that Tracy was right, and he needed a babysitter to carry him through. The other voice said it was too early to make a call, and he'd never know if he didn't try. It was a classic devil-and-angel-on-the-shoulders argument that only frustrated him more.

He looked up at the sound of Shawn's truck rumbling to life, and waved as he pulled out. Shawn nodded back, one hand busy on the steering wheel and the other holding a cellphone to his ear.

CHAPTER EIGHT

Tracy stood up in her stirrups and slipped her ringing phone out of her back pocket.

"Hello?" she answered as she settled back into the saddle.

"Are you still looking for a header?"

A grin broke across her face, and the caller needed no introduction. "I sure am, Shawn. Way to leave me hanging, though. I was beginning to think you weren't going to call."

"I can't come to Foremost to practice, and I'm still gonna run with Carson in Coalhurst, but I'll head for you too, if you want."

Splitting his time between two teams wasn't ideal, but it also came as no surprise. Shawn was one of those fiercely loyal guys; once he gave his word, he stuck to it, which was probably why he still gave her the time of day. Goodness knows, she didn't deserve his friendship.

"I can live with that."

"Does Carson know you're going to rope with me?"

"Doesn't really matter, I didn't promise anything beyond Coalhurst. And, honestly, he was pretty shaken after today's practice. I really don't think he's going to last. He's rusty. I mean *really* rusty. I feel for him, Trace. I just don't know if he's got what it takes."

A smirk inched its way across her face. *Good.* Served him and Vince right for trying to tell her he would stand in the way of what she wanted.

"Good. That'll get me one step closer to my goal."

"By destroying a guy's dreams? I thought you liked him, Trace."

"I don't."

"You liked him enough to leave with him."

"I was attracted to him. There's a difference."

Silence met her ears. Shawn never did seem to know how to handle her. He was a decent guy; he cared for others and was always willing to lend a helping hand. And despite how decent he was, Tracy wouldn't give him the time of day. He deserved a much nicer woman than her. Someone less self-involved, and less driven. Someone who would stare at him with adoring eyes and appreciate him for his kind heart, not take advantage of it.

"I'll see you on Friday, then."

"Yeah."

She pulled the phone away from her face to hang up, then paused, and brought it back to her ear. "Shawn?"

"Yeah."

"Thank you. You didn't have to do this."

"Is that a formal thank you from the great Tracy Miller?"

She could feel the heat of a blush spreading across her face. "Don't get used to it. I don't say it often, and it's pretty unlikely you'll ever hear it again."

"Bye, Trace."

She hung up, standing in the stirrups to slip the phone back into her pocket before nudging Jack forward into a trot down the fence line she'd been checking previously.

She never had to look back at her life before, or really thought about how she treated people. Her life had always been about striving to be the toughest and best at everything. She didn't get to where she was by making many apologies, or accepting help from others. It's not that she wasn't thankful for the help she received, but she would've turned it down if she thought she could do it on her own. If she could have done singles roping, she would have. But she didn't know a single woman who possessed enough strength to bring down a steer on her own, at least, not in the time required for a rodeo competition.

Now that she was back to where she had started as a teen, and fighting to get on top as quickly as possible, something told Tracy she'd have to kiss some of her pride goodbye. Apologies would have to be spoken, help would have to be accepted, and she'd have a good number of people to thank by the end of it all.

At least her mom taught her how to be gracious when necessary. Her dad's genes seemed much stronger in her, though. The urge to fight, well, everything, and to rise in self-defense, how failure was not an option, all that came from her dad. The difference between Tracy and her father, though, was when his dreams were dashed, he gave up. He just accepted it as the end of his career. Tracy refused to believe she was done.

I'm not so different from Carson, she thought, before shaking her head to dislodge it. She was *very* different from him. She'd been doing this all her life. She knew she had the skill and ability to make it back to the top. Carson had a dream, a horse, and a distinct lack of skill. That would get him nothing but disappointment.

* * *

Lying in bed that night, Tracy ran her hand across her brace. She made an appointment with a doc in Lethbridge the following day to see about getting a clean bill of health. Her hand was doing well, at least by her standards. It didn't ache anymore, and she needed better wrist movement if she hoped to rope.

She managed to push the problem of her sprained hand behind her when she still didn't have a partner, but the rodeo was coming up fast, and now that she had a header, her hand had to be dealt with as soon as possible. It wasn't like she was any stranger to injury. She just never had that kind of pressure to get back in the game before she was fully healed.

Turning over in her bed, she sighed, and looked at the clock. It shone 12:30 a.m. at her. She'd been lying in bed for over two hours now, and hadn't even begun to drift off. Sitting up, she flicked on the light next to her bed and let her feet fall over the side. They touched the cold linoleum floor. She ran her hand through her hair, her fingers catching in the snarls. One of the downsides to having curly hair was trying to keep it smooth and contained. Braiding was a necessity.

She got up and walked across the trailer, hitting the start button on the coffee maker. She got it all ready to go before climbing into bed every night so that it required only minimal effort in the morning. She listened to it brew, sitting at the booth of the kitchen table and staring outside at her horse, illuminated by the moonlight.

The sound of crickets and frogs hypnotized her, and she leaned across the table, resting her head on her arm. Her eyes grew heavy, and the steady sound of brewing coffee only enhanced the symphony that lulled her to welcomed sleep.

* * *

The blaring sound of her alarm clock woke Tracy and she blinked and sat up. Her arm felt fat and tingled from loss of circulation after sleeping on it all night. She rubbed her eyes and gasped at the pain that shot through from her fingers to her shoulder. Her nerves felt like they were suddenly on fire.

Cold coffee from the night before filled the small, four-cup coffee brewer. She walked over and picked up the pot, before sniffing it and wrinkling her nose. *Iced coffee? Or dump it and brew fresh?* She toyed with the idea, since she hated to waste anything. Eventually, she turned to her right and dumped the pot in the sink anyway. Iced coffee was great and all, but not meant for mornings.

No, the only thing that would do for mornings was hot, fresh, black coffee, preferably strong and thick.

She tapped her fingers on the counter as she waited for it to brew.

A knock sounded on her trailer door before it popped open. Vince peeked in.

"Good morning."

"Don't sound so chipper, I haven't had my coffee yet."

"Sorry, but I'm off to Foremost to grab some supplies. You around today?"

"Nope, I've got a doctor's appointment in Lethbridge."

"Okay, good luck."

That was it, short and sweet. Vince's head disappeared and her trailer door latched, leaving her alone to drink her coffee in peace.

The light came on and she poured her coffee into a mug. She cradled it between her hands and sat down at her table and watched some birds flitting about the yard. The rumble of Vince's red, diesel truck scattered the birds, but when it pulled out, they returned to their previous positions.

Checking her phone, Tracy sighed. *Time to get ready.* She had to drive nearly two hours to Lethbridge, and her appointment was scheduled in two-and-a-half. She removed her brace and jumped into the tiny, closet-like shower, closing her eyes as the hot steam ran over her. She faced the shower head, so the hot water could massage the sweaty skin that was covered by her brace. Yep, she couldn't wait to get rid of the disgusting thing.

She quickly washed her hair with one hand and rinsed; she wasn't about to strain her hand; and certainly not right before seeing the doctor. But what she wouldn't have done for a full-sized shower, or better yet, a bath. Maybe a toilet that wasn't plastic, too. She loved her life on the road, but there was a certain appeal to a brick and mortar house that every once in a while called to her. *Maybe something for the winter months.* She just didn't know where… or when she'd be ready for that.

She pasted on a smile and climbed out. Ten minutes later, her brace on, dressed and ready, she poured coffee into a travel mug and climbed into her truck. Driving up Highway 641, she turned right onto Highway 61 toward Lethbridge. She followed the Red Coat Trail for an hour with nothing but fields and hills all around her, until she turned onto AB-4 into Lethbridge. After another half hour fighting morning traffic, she pulled up outside the hospital.

She parked and strode through the busy, sterile-smelling building. Pausing at a reception desk, she pulled out her health card and waited for some attention.

"Can I help you?"

"I have an appointment with Dr. Hadley."

She handed the health card over and waited as the receptionist studied her computer screen. She returned the card to Tracy and said, "You can take a seat."

Tracy nodded and found an empty seat in the already busy waiting room. *I'm going to be here all day.* She glanced around, leaned back and stretched her legs forward, crossing one worn cowboy boot over the other. Reclining, she pulled her hat over her face, and closed her eyes. *Might as well catch up on some sleep.* Despite falling asleep almost as soon as she sat down at her table last night, she woke up feeling unrested and sore.

"Tracy Miller?"

She lifted her hat. "Here."

"Sorry to cut your nap short—"

"So am I."

The nurse standing over her with a clipboard glared. It was a practiced glare that had even Tracy sitting a little straighter in her seat. "There are plenty of people here who would gladly take your spot if you'd rather nap."

If the woman hadn't been glowering at Tracy, and making her feel like the wallpaper behind her was wilting, Tracy might have taken her up on it. But the woman had a way of making her feel like she should tighten her belt, stand up straight, and ride that pony… Had she been in an arena rather than a hospital waiting room. She stood up and followed the nurse into a tiny examination room.

"The doctor will be right with you. Feel free to nap while you wait."

Tracy nodded, and sat down, setting her hat on the chair beside her. She inspected her fingernails, picking the dirt out from underneath each one in turn, and then starting over again.

Standing up, she began to pace. *They show me into a room and then leave me here to twiddle my thumbs.* She hated doctors. She hated hospitals. But most of all, she hated being injured.

The door sprung open and in walked the doctor. "Good morning, Tracy, my name is Chris Hadley," greeted her doctor. He had blond hair that was wavy and a little messy, like he styled it by running his fingers through it in the morning. It was thinning a little at the top, but that was barely noticeable. He wore thick, black, plastic-rimmed glasses that made her think of Clark Kent, nerdy, but attractive in his own way. Maybe it was the dimples, or his piercing blue eyes with little laugh lines at the corners—or how he exuded youthfulness, despite being, Tracy would guess, somewhere in his mid-thirties.

"Morning," she replied. She stopped her pacing and crossed her arms over her chest, bending one leg to hold the majority of her weight and, in doing so, cocking a hip out as if to say she didn't want any nonsense today. Or, at least, she hoped to convey that concept.

"How's the hand? Your chart says it's a sprain with some bruising?"

The doctor swiveled in his chair to face her and looked up, meeting her eyes.

"Yeah, this brace needs to go."

He frowned. "Let's take a look."

He removed her brace and began a few stretches. Up, down, and squeezing certain points. With each movement, he asked if it hurt.

"Nope," she responded dutifully, despite some slight discomfort. She willed her face to remain blank and refused to wince.

He let her hand go with a smile. "If there's no pain, I think we can safely say you've healed up nicely. But keep the brace. If you feel any pain, put it back on and come see me."

He stood up and walked with her to the door, which he opened. He let her walk through, but he remained in the doorway. "And Tracy, stay out of trouble. I'd prefer not to see you in my exam room."

"Believe me, I'd prefer to see less of you as well," she said, followed by a chuckle.

"Now, don't say that."

"Did I hurt your feelings, Dr. Hadley?"

"Chris, please. And yes, it does sting a little when a beautiful woman says she wants to see less of me."

"You said it first," she challenged, meeting his eyes.

"I only meant in the context of injury. I'd like to see more of you, *outside* the hospital."

Tracy cringed and shook her head. "No, sorry. I don't date doctors."

"I'm not asking you to date me, I'm asking you to go on *a* date with me. Just one."

She shook her head again, and her eyes locked with his. She wasn't afraid to stand her ground and fight her battles. Chris was nothing she couldn't handle. She wrestled with animals weighing over half a ton, and an insistent man didn't intimidate her in the least.

"No."

"One drink."

"No."

He offered her a less-than-genuine smile and shrugged. "You'll change your mind. Have a nice day, Tracy."

She raised an eyebrow, surprised by his unflagging confidence. Putting her hat back on, she began walking down the hall, her boots making a unique clomp that echoed loudly with each step.

He's not my type, she told herself, but for some reason, she found herself stopping anyway.

"Forget something?" he asked.

She didn't turn around. What did she have to lose? Sure, he wasn't her *usual* type, but she hadn't gotten very far with the men she dated up until now anyway. Maybe she should mix things up a little.

"I'm not saying yes. But I'll be roping in the Coalhurst Rodeo on Saturday. If you happen to find yourself there, I might be convinced to grab a bite to eat and a beer."

She looked over her shoulder before leaving, catching Chris's smile. *He better be smiling,* she thought. It's not often Tracy Miller changes her mind about anything.

CHAPTER NINE

The Coalhurst rodeo grounds buzzed with activity as Carson pulled up in his truck and trailer on Friday morning. Other rigs pulled in and parked, before men and women in Wranglers and cowboy hats, or ball caps, off-loaded their horses and led them to their rented stalls.

Driving up to the rider area, he put his truck in park and jumped out, walking to the first person he saw wearing a reflective vest.

"Hey, can I get some directions? Not too sure where to go."

The rodeo volunteer looked down at his clipboard. "Name?"

"Carson Walker. I've got a stall and trailer spot booked."

The guy ran his finger down a list, then flipped a few pages over. "Ah, here you are. Walker, Carson."

"Yeah, that's what I said."

"Last name first, son. Okay, you're in stall eight, block C. Trailer parking is behind the stall setups, just pick a free spot and set 'er up.

"Thanks."

Driving around the stall blocks, Carson pulled up beside another trailer and parked. His rig didn't have the nice living quarters that so many others did. He simply had a mattress in the gooseneck portion of the trailer and a camping stove in his truck. That would have to do for now. He just hoped the temperature didn't drop too much overnight, or he'd be a little chilled. His stock trailer didn't have much in the way of protection from the elements. Open slats ran along the entire length of the trailer, including the tack storage room where his makeshift sleeping quarters were located.

He unloaded Danny-boy and led him to the stall the volunteer designated. There wasn't much to the place; a simple small town rodeo with old, metal stalls that had seen much better days. The doors took some muscle to get open and closed. The floor was bare dirt and they didn't even provide any water pails. It was self-boarding all the way here. Three walls, a door, and a parking stall. That was the rodeo life.

Why am I chasing this? he thought as Danny entered the stall. He unclipped the lead and muscled the door closed again. *There is nothing glamorous about this life. Nothing.*

He spent all week, hour-upon-hour, trying to maximize his timing on the ground. That way, when Shawn came in the evening, Carson would be ready to do it mounted. On Tuesday, he missed a few times, but was definitely becoming more consistent. And on Wednesday and Thursday, he managed to catch almost every single one. Now it was just speed that he needed to build up. He liked to think he had a chance at placing this weekend, however slim. He *needed* to think that, otherwise why was he even there?

It took a while to get everything settled. He opened a straw bale and shook it out over the middle of the stall. Danny would spread the rest. Picking up the ten-gallon pail from inside the trailer, he waited in line at the hose to fill it up.

"Carson?"

He hefted the pail up and turned around. The blond hair tamed by a braid beneath a beat-up cowboy hat gave away her identity before he even looked at her face.

"Tracy."

He looked down at her hand. No brace. That could only mean she'd be roping. Against him. He tipped his hat toward her and kept walking.

"I hear we share a roping partner."

Carson stopped. He ground his teeth together and closed his eyes. She was just trying to get a rise out of him, that was all. Shawn would have told him that he agreed to rope with Tracy, right?

"He didn't tell you?"

Carson didn't turn around, but closed his eyes, took a deep breath, and let it out slowly. "Doesn't matter. It's not like it affects me anyway."

He heard her walking up behind him, and her hand rested on his shoulder and trailed down his arm in a teasing way that immediately brought him back to the night he kissed her. It left him frozen in place, paralyzed by errant thoughts.

She circled around to face him. "I can't believe he didn't tell you. It's like I'm his dirty, little secret…" she trailed off, then a slight smile curled at her lips, looking more malicious than friendly. "Maybe because he knows he'll win with me."

"Don't get ahead of yourself." What he wouldn't do to wipe that smug look off her face. But he had to keep his cool. She wanted to get a rise out of him, and he refused to give her the satisfaction.

"You drew an earlier run than me, you know."

"So?"

"That makes you the practice run for Shawn."

She flipped her braid over her shoulder and walked away, leaving him standing there, unsure what just transpired between them.

She's just trying to rattle me, he thought, walking back to the stall block. The problem was: it worked. He was rattled, and pissed that Shawn didn't tell him before. The water sloshed out of the pail and onto his pant leg, drenching his calf all the way down to his boots.

"Crap!"

"Need help?"

He looked up and saw Shawn. Great, just the person he wanted to see.

"Everyone is showing up at the same time and place," he muttered, walking into Danny's stall.

"Well, that's what people do at rodeos."

He hung the pail up and turned back to face Shawn. "Something you want to tell me?"

"What?"

"Maybe a dirty, little secret?"

Shawn frowned and shook his head. "What are you talking about?"

"Maybe if I put it this way, you'll understand; anything you want to tell me about a certain tall, blond, and beautiful woman?"

"Oh."

"Yes, 'oh'. Slipped your mind?"

"Didn't think it mattered."

Carson shrugged. "It's not 'cause I'm your," he paused, "*practice run?*"

Shawn smiled. "Sorry, man, no such luck. I can't say no to that woman. Never could. It has absolutely nothing to do with you and everything to do with her. It's *always* about her."

"So I'm figuring out."

Shawn slapped the top of the stall and nodded. "I'm going to get settled in. Just steer clear of Tracy, okay? I know something went on between you two, but if you're smart, you'll avoid getting caught in that woman's trap."

"Like you did?"

"I got caught long before I was smart enough to see through her."

He walked away, leaving Carson alone. Or as alone as he could be amongst the bustling activity that comprised the rodeo. There wouldn't be any issue of him being snared by Tracy. He'd already seen through her, and didn't like what he saw.

* * *

"Hey, Carson, you coming to Billy's?" asked Shawn, walking up to where he sat in a lawn chair. His feet were thrown up on a small, fold-up table and a beer was open beside him.

"Billy's?"

"Yeah, the bar. A bunch of us are going there for supper."

"Tracy going to be there?"

"Of course. But there will be plenty of other people there. You won't even have to look at her, much less make conversation."

"Sure, why not?"

"I'll give you a ride."

Carson's feet dropped off the table and he chugged back the last few sips of beer in the bottom of the bottle. "Okay, I'm ready."

The drive only took about sixty seconds, grand total, up the main street to the only bar in town. Coalhurst was a home away from home. The bar was even attached to a motel. They could have been driving through the streets of Foremost if he didn't know better.

He followed Shawn into the packed bar. He wasn't kidding when he said everyone would be there. People wearing jeans, cowboy boots, and hats were crammed everywhere. They were all talking over each other and shouting to be heard, which soon had Carson's head spinning a little. He preferred quiet, intimate settings over this.

"I'm going to grab a drink at the bar."

"There's a free table in the corner. I'll be there, then we can order some food."

Carson nodded his consent, not really wanting to shout over the noise again, before pushing through the crowd of people to the worn, wooden bar.

He managed to make his way to the front and leaned over the bar, trying to grab the attention of the bartender. One whisked by. "I'll be right with you," he shouted, his hands full of another drink order.

"I'll have an MGD," sounded a distinctly female voice from the other end of the bar.

The guy who just told Carson he'd be with him, stopped his progress and turned to the beer fridge under the counter. After pulling out the requested MGD and popping off the top, he slid it over to none other than Tracy. Carson gritted his teeth together. *Why can't you just walk out of my life?*

He waited for the bartender to return and take his order, but patience got him nowhere. Ten minutes later, he was still waiting while people all around him got served. He felt a hand on his shoulder and looked over to see Tracy. Her touch sent tingles down his arm and through his chest. As much as he disliked her, his body reacted exactly the opposite. He couldn't deny the attraction there.

It's just physical.

"You need to be a little more forceful, cowboy. If you stand here waiting to be served, you'll be here all night."

"Why do you always have to butt into my business?"

She laughed. "What do you want?"

"A Keith's Red."

"Hey, Billy, Keith's Red over here!" shouted Tracy.

The bartender who promised Carson service, but never made it over, nodded, and immediately went to the beer fridge.

"You know that only works because you're a woman."

"And I make myself known."

Billy walked over and handed Carson the beer. "That'll be six dollars and fifty cents."

He handed him a ten and slipped a couple of quarters into the tip jar when he got his change. He turned to find the table where Shawn said he'd be sitting.

"No *thank you* for getting you the drink?" she asked as she followed him through the crowd.

"Thanks."

"You here alone?"

"Nope." *Just go away.*

"Shawn!" she shouted right next to his ear. He looked over to see her waving at Shawn, who was sitting at the table. She pushed past him, her braid bouncing playfully from side-to-side. *Great, now she's here to stay.*

Carson followed her to the table and grabbed the empty seat across from her, putting as much distance between them as he could.

"So, Carson, ready for tomorrow?"

"As ready as I'll ever be." He took a sip of his beer.

"Nerves are normal, you know. I'm sure you'll do fine. Shawn, here, is a great roper."

He frowned, studying her. She did a complete three-sixty and he couldn't put a finger on her. One minute, she tried to make him feel inferior; and the next, she was offering him encouragement. He couldn't hate this Tracy, but he sure despised the other one. *So which one are you now?*

"Of course, he's roping with me too, so you'll have to settle for second place."

And there it was; the sting of her words.

"You just can't be nice, can you? You have to add some insult just to raise yourself up."

"I *am* being nice. Second place for a greenhorn is nothing to scoff at, and I think maybe you might just have a chance."

"You wouldn't know. You've never seen me rope."

"Guys, settle down," cut in Shawn.

"Look, I was just trying to be nice, but if you're going to be such a *sensitive girl* about it, I'll just leave you alone."

Tracy pushed back her chair and got up, leaving her empty beer bottle on the table.

"I've got the practice arena booked for seven a.m., Shawn. You'll be there?"

"Yep."

She flounced off, her braid still swinging, but this time in an angry motion. How in the world could a simple braid tell so much about her state of mind?

Carson took a sip of his beer rend picked up the menu just as the waitress approached them.

"You guys had enough time with the menus?"

Shawn nodded. "Yeah, I'm ready to order. Carson?"

"You order; I'll be ready in a second."

"I'll take the double-decker burger, fries, and gravy."

"Perfect. And for you?" She turned to look at Carson.

He folded up the menu that he had barely started to read. "I'll just have the same."

"I'll bring those out shortly. Can I get you any drinks while you wait?"

"I'll have a Coors," said Shawn, who was sipping on water up until now.

"I'm good." Carson still had half a beer left and wanted to have all his wits about him in the morning. Shawn appeared to be of the same frame of mind.

But Tracy didn't seem to be thinking that way. His lips turned up in a smile. She had at least one beer before he ran into her, and then finished another at their table. He looked around the bar, spotting her by the pool table. She was holding a cue in one hand and a beer in the other. *That has to be her third, at least.* And the night was still young. So unless she planned on heading out soon, which didn't seem too likely, at the pace she was going, she could be in for a very rough morning.

Shawn was just the kind of company Carson liked. He didn't talk much, but sat contentedly watching all the goings on around them. That left Carson free to keep an eye on Tracy.

"Did you book the chute?" asked Shawn.

He didn't take his attention off Tracy, but nodded. "Yeah, um, eight-forty-five; we have it."

"Good, that gives me a break between you and Tracy."

"Yep."

The waitress walked up with a tray full of drinks, and placed a bottle of Coors in front of Shawn. "Here you go. Your food should be out in five minutes or so."

"Thanks."

Carson nodded at her. "Hey, can I order a drink?"

"Sure, what'll you have?"

"An MGD, and send it to the blond woman playing pool."

She looked over and squinted, as if it would help her see through the dim lighting and sea of cowboy hats. "The one with the braid?"

"That's her."

"I'll bring that right out."

She walked away and he turned to look at Shawn. Shawn was frowning, one hand on his beer that he hadn't even taken a sip from.

"What are you doing?"

"Buying her a drink."

"Yeah, why?"

He shrugged. "Peace offering. I figured if we're going to run in the same circles, we might as well be friends."

"You're asking for trouble, you know that, right?"

"I'm just sick of fighting," he lied, but he couldn't hold back the smile that broke through.

"You better think twice about going to war with Trace. I've never known her to lose."

"You don't know me."

He looked over to see the waitress delivering the drink to Tracy. She pointed at Carson, and he tipped his hat, raising his glass in salute. Tracy smiled and nodded back at him before taking a sip of the beer. If she suspected he was up to no good, she didn't show it.

A little later, their burgers arrived, along with another Keith's Red.

"From Tracy," she said with a wink. The waitress obviously thought there was some flirtation going on. If only she knew.

"Thanks."

Tracy had no idea what she started. If she hoped to outdrink him, she could keep dreaming.

He raised his bottle to her and took a sip, then turned away. Putting down the beer, he gripped the messy burger with two hands. He had to squeeze it as tightly as he could to bite into all the layers, but it was delicious. Nothing could beat bar food, especially with a beer to wash it down.

"Trouble this way comes," said Shawn around a mouthful of food.

Carson looked over his shoulder to see Tracy sauntering up.

"Hey, boys," she said, taking a seat and reaching over to steal a fry from Carson's plate.

"You're welcome," he muttered.

"Oh, and thanks for the beer," she added, smiling as she bit into the fry.

"Consider it a peace offering."

"That's very... mature of you."

How could she make even mature sound like an insult?

"Yeah well, thanks for reciprocating."

"Nothing to bond friendship like drinking together."

He nodded, biting into his burger again so he didn't have to say anything to her.

Silence fell over the table. Shawn seemed to be working very hard at keeping his eyes downcast.

Tracy slapped her hand on the table. "I know, let's do shots!"

"Not a good idea, Trace. We have an early start tomorrow."

"It's just a shot, Shawn. Don't be such a killjoy."

Shawn sighed, and Tracy seemed to take that as consent because she got up. "I'll be right back." She left with a bounce in her step that made her look downright gleeful.

"You seriously have no idea what you started. After this shot that she insists we take, I'm leaving."

Carson had to agree. "Yeah, I'm with you. She doesn't need my help taking things too far tonight."

She came back with a tray full of shots.

"What is that?" asked Shawn, his eyes wide.

"Shots."

"That's a lot of shots. I thought you meant one each! Not..." he stopped and started pointing at each glass as he silently counted. "Seriously? Three each?"

Carson sat back, watching the exchange between the two friends who grew up together.

"Loosen up, Shawn. Normally, you'd be all over this."

"Not the night before a competition." He sighed. "I'm out of here. If you two want to sabotage your chances of winning, be my guest. I, for one, choose to be smart."

"Guess that just leaves you and me, Carson."

He shook his head. "Sorry, but Shawn is my ride."

"We can walk. The rodeo grounds are only a couple blocks away."

Shawn was already standing at the counter, paying his bill. If Carson wanted that ride, he had to leave now. Tracy picked up a shot glass and slid it over to him.

"You aren't going to leave me alone with all these drinks, are you?"

He shrugged and picked up the shot. "Guess not." What did he have to worry about? He was bigger, heavier, and she already had more to drink than him. She'd be down for the count long before he would. And she'd definitely be off her game tomorrow, leaving him to take the top spot and score the most points.

"Cheers."

He clinked glasses with her and threw back the straight whiskey.

Tracy slid another toward him.

"Don't you think we should pace ourselves? You've already had a fair bit."

"Not man enough to drink with me?"

"I'm just concerned that you're going to overdo it. Like Shawn said, we have to be fresh and ready tomorrow."

"Pretty sure that wasn't a concern on your mind when you bought me the beer earlier."

She threw back the whiskey, not waiting for him to join her with the drink.

"I told you, that was a peace offering."

"That was an attempt to sabotage me," she snapped.

"You seem to be doing a good enough job of that all on your own."

"Sorry I disappoint you."

Where did that come from? Why does my opinion matter to her at all?

"You don't disappoint me." He let out a little chuckle. "Heck, you intimidate me, Tracy."

"Good." She slid a shot to him. "You need to catch up."

Carson matched her shot-for-shot, but after only a couple more, his vision began to swim. His better judgement told him he had to call it a night.

"We better head back."

Tracy nodded, getting up and swaying before grabbing the back of a chair to gain her balance.

"Here," he offered the crook of his elbow.

"You're aaalways such a gentlemaaan," she slurred, annunciating words in all the wrong spots. "Opening doorssss, offering aaaarms."

"I like to be the knight in shining armor," he whispered.

"I don't need reeeescuing."

"I know."

He led her to the bar, while concentrating on walking in a straight line. He had to also support Tracy, who was definitely in worse shape than he was.

Paying both tabs, he led her down the long abandoned roads to the rodeo grounds. The walk took a lot longer than it should have as they wove across the sidewalk, but eventually, they stumbled back to the trailers in one piece.

"Where is your trailer?"

"That way," she slurred, pointing unsteadily in the general direction of the arena, not toward the group of trailers.

He sighed and started walking through the middle of them all, hoping he'd spot hers. After wandering up a few aisles unsuccessfully, he spotted hers at the back right corner of the makeshift camping area. As he turned to head in that direction, Tracy stumbled. The cool evening air did a lot to sober up Carson, but she seemed to have hit the point of no return. He picked her up, and carried her, holding her tightly against his chest. With some fumbling and muttering under his breath, he managed to open her trailer without having to put her down. He carried her in, ducking through the doorway to allow clearance for his tall frame. These RVs were not made for his height.

Tracy snored in his arms, already sound asleep, and he smiled as he lowered her onto her bed. He threw her hat on the table and pulled off her boots, placing them on the floor beside her bed.

"Good night, Tracy," he whispered.

She stirred a little. "I'm gonna kick your butt tomorrow," she replied before returning to sleep.

He let out a laugh. She wasn't in any shape to kick anybody's butt now, and probably wouldn't be doing much better tomorrow. She looked so peaceful, though, that it struck a chord with him. He could see through the armor she wore to hide the damage lying underneath.

"What made you this way, Tracy?" he whispered, brushing a strand of hair away from her face. He left the trailer and latched the door securely behind him.

CHAPTER TEN

Tracy blindly fumbled for the snooze button on her alarm. The blaring was instantly silenced, and she looked over at the clock.

"Crap!" She sat up, eyes wide, instantly awake. Then the headache hit. The pounding was right behind her eyes. It was like someone turned up the bass inside her head with no escape.

She groaned, lying back down. *Why am I still wearing my clothes?*

Digging into her pocket, she pulled out her phone, and flipped it open. Squinting at the numbers, she read 8:12 AM. The alarm clock didn't lie. She missed her seven a.m. practice with Shawn—*He's gonna kill me.*

What was I thinking last night? Overdoing it like that? It was supposed to be fun; just burning off the steam that was building up over the past few weeks. She felt good. Then Carson walked in. All six-foot-and-then-some of him, and she immediately felt drawn to him like a magnet.

He started the war; she just accepted the challenge by refusing to back down. It wasn't one of her brightest shining moments, but it sure beat punching someone in the face.

A knock sounded on the door and Tracy got up. Opening it, she had to squint against the bright morning sunlight. Speak of the devil; Carson stood there, his hat protecting his eyes.

"I took your practice slot this morning. Figured you wouldn't be awake yet."

"Guess I deserve that."

"If you hurry, you can have my eight-forty-five slot."

She blinked and shook her head. *Am I hearing him right?* "What?"

"You can have my slot. Even you need practice."

"Uh, thank you."

"Don't mention it. Seriously. I feel like a bit of a fool for last night. I was childish."

"You aren't alone in that. Thanks for, uh, getting me home."

"You're welcome."

He stood there, his hands in his pockets and shoulders hunched while looking down at his toes as he kicked the dirt. He looked bashful. If she could have seen his face, she'd have bet money on some pink filling his cheeks.

"I better get ready. I'll see you later."

"Later." He tipped his hat and walked away.

Closing the door, she sighed. Food and coffee to go while she got Jack saddled was what she needed. Turning around, she started with the coffee, getting it brewing before throwing together a sandwich. Going into the cupboard, she found a bottle of aspirin and quickly downed a couple.

Coffee was almost ready, so she slipped into her bathroom to brush her teeth, scrubbing away while walking into the kitchen before spitting into the sink, and rinsing. She sloshed some coffee on the counter and the floor as she filled a travel mug, and dropped a tea towel on the floor, mopping the spill with her foot. She found her boots beside her bed, which she pulled on; and with her sandwich in her mouth, and coffee in hand, she clomped down the steps.

The aspirin began to take effect as she wolfed down her PB and J sandwich on the way to Jack's stall. She sipped coffee between bites to help wash it down.

Saddling Jack, Tracy slipped his bridle over his ears and took the reins, leading him out of the stall with her coffee cup in her other hand.

At the practice arena, a team was just finishing up their run. She walked up next to Shawn, who waited next to the in gate.

"Morning," she said, plastering on a smile.

"You missed our practice," he said, his voice even and flat.

"Yeah, sorry about that." She did her best to sound cheerful, but Shawn was definitely pissed, and she hated making him mad.

"You're lucky Carson gave us his slot."

"I know." She didn't know what else to say. It was the truth; she *was* lucky. But she hated knowing it was due to Carson being a stand-up guy. She didn't want to see him that way. She wanted to hate him, and see him as nothing more than competition. He made it really hard when he was nice, especially when she didn't deserve it. "You know we don't need to practice, though. We can still wipe this arena clean on a cold run."

Shawn sighed, turning to face her. "Enough with the act, Trace! You're not better than everyone else, and you had better stop with the attitude, or you'll never find another roping partner."

"*Excuse* me." She put her arms up in mock surrender.

"We haven't roped together in years. You think we can just enter a team sport and expect to win? You're dreaming! We need every minute of the half hour practice we have booked, and the sooner you get that through your head, the better."

Tracy raised her eyebrows, fully taken aback. Shawn was usually laid back, happy-go-lucky, and eager to treat her like the world revolved around her. Something had to be bothering him for him to get like that.

They waited in silence for their turn. When it finally came, Tracy mounted and rode without a word. She couldn't bring herself to talk to him. The air between them seemed electrified with Shawn's seething.

The chute sprang open and they took off. The first run went well, but not perfectly. She couldn't deny they needed the practice. Problem was, if they won, she'd have to thank Carson for it. And she hated that.

* * *

The smell of fried food and the sound of voices filled the arena as Tracy stood outside the gate. Carson and Shawn were up next. She climbed up the chute, hanging over the edge next to Shawn.

"Hey, good luck out there," she said, smiling.

"Just don't come in first?" asked Carson.

"Don't worry, you won't. That spot is reserved for me." She winked.

"We'll see," responded Carson, smiling. Whatever could be said about last night, at least they buried the hatchet for now.

The chute sprang open and the horses and riders sprang to life, chasing down the steer that made a mad dash for the other side of the arena. Tracy watched the ropes spinning through the air. Carson's technique was definitely there. She watched his rope arch over the steer and catch it, tightening around his neck. The steer began to buck, freeing up a foot for Shawn.

"Five point five seconds to Shawn Dalton and Carson Walker!"

Not bad for a first competitive run together. Not bad at all, especially considering Shawn's strengths didn't lie in heeling. Carson was good, though. Rusty, like Shawn said, but he definitely had potential. He needed more practice, but with the right partner, he could do really well.

"Great run," she said as they led their horses out.

"Yeah, definitely not bad," responded Shawn.

"Ready to do that again?"

"Yep."

Carson kept walking, leaving them behind. He didn't utter a single word as Tracy and Shawn conversed behind him.

"Hey! You coming back to watch?" she called out.

He turned around, walking backwards, and nodded.

There were three more teams before she and Shawn rode.

They watched the competitors, side-by-side, holding their horses that stood quietly and calmly behind them. The pool of talent here wasn't bad, but Tracy was pretty sure Shawn and Carson would manage to place with their time.

"We're up," said Shawn, climbing off the fence and walking over to the chute.

Tracy followed. Mounted and waiting inside the arena next to the chute, she went through her ritual. She checked her hat, making sure it was on snugly, then ran her gloved hands up and down the reins until she found the perfect length. It was all in the feel. She needed enough to give Jack cues with only the slightest movement, but also enough freedom to do what he did best: chasing cattle.

She clenched her fist around the rope. Squeezing each finger tighter in turn, then loosening her grip.

"Trace?"

She looked over at Shawn.

"Good?"

She nodded and leaned forward in the saddle.

The chute sprang open.

Jack burst forward like a spring released from its confines.

Her rope flew into the air, circling once, twice, three times.

Shawn's rope arched and circled the steer's head, pulling tight around both horns.

The steer bucked. Once. Twice. His back feet flying into the air, Tracy let her rope go, and then yanked as it fell perfectly around both back feet.

The steer went down.

"Five point two seconds!"

Tracy pumped her fist and grinned broadly at Shawn.

"That gives us our time to beat. Great run by Shawn Dalton and Tracy Miller."

They dismounted and walked out.

"That was a really great run," greeted Carson outside. He didn't look that thrilled, though.

"Hey, chin up. You'll probably still place," said Tracy.

"Yeah, thanks."

"Tracy!"

She frowned, looking for who called her name.

"Oh, no," she muttered upon seeing the mop of wavy, blond hair making its way through the crowd toward her. "I can't believe he actually came."

"Hey, Tracy, you did awesome!"

"Hi, Chris."

"Hey, I'm Shawn." He outstretched his hand in greeting, intercepting Chris before he could reach Tracy. Chris accepted the handshake. Tracy watched. It was friendly, amicable, and not something she was used to seeing from Shawn when meeting her guy friends; not that Chris could really be called that.

"Carson."

Their handshake was not the same. It seemed to have a battle of the wills mixed in. The men locked eyes, Chris had to look up to meet Carson's, and Tracy looked down to see his white knuckles. *Was he seriously trying to out-squeeze a farm boy?*

Chris's hand fell to his side and he clenched his fist a few times, then shook out his hand. Tracy watched in silent amusement. Good, someone needed to put him in his place. Of course, since that someone was Carson, it brought up a whole different set of concerns. Like, why in the world Carson felt so territorial over her. Did it have something to do with him rescuing her last night? Or was it out of some bro-code with Shawn?

"I, uh, I gotta put my horse away," she said, looking for a way to escape the awkward silence that descended upon the four of them.

"I'll come with you," said Chris.

"Sorry, non-riders aren't allowed back there. Come with me, we'll go grab a table by the concessions and wait for Tracy," said Carson.

Tracy looked at him and frowned, trying to catch his gaze, but he refused to meet her eyes. First the handshake, now a lie to keep Chris away from her.

"Oh, okay."

"I better put my girl away too. See you in a bit," said Shawn.

Tracy and Shawn fell into step with each other.

"Who's the guy?"

"My doctor."

"He seems awfully... friendly."

"Yeah, a little too friendly. He wouldn't take no as an answer when he asked me for a date, so I put him off by saying I had this rodeo to compete in. I never thought he'd actually come."

Shawn nodded and stopped outside Tracy's stall, letting her walk Jack in, before he leaned on the gate. "Look, Trace, I'm not going to continue partnering with you."

She looked up. "Why not? We had a great run."

"Yeah, we did. And I had a good run with Carson. But I have a job and a life beyond rodeos. And, quite frankly, I'm done chasing you. You're never going to go for me, so why should I put my life on hold for you, you know?"

She nodded, undoing the latigo on her saddle.

"I don't know what is going on between you and Carson, but there is definitely something beyond competition, friendly or not."

She scoffed. "Carson? Really?"

"And then this Chris guy shows up. I'm just not willing to be a part of some love triangle, or square, or whatever you have going on."

"There is no love anything. There is nothing between Carson and me, or Chris and me. And you... you always knew nothing was ever going to happen with us."

"I know that, but what I'm wondering is, why do you keep stringing me along?"

His eyes looked sad, defeated. So he finally realized after all these years. She tried telling him, and paraded other guys in front of him, and he finally figured it out. But instead of relief, a sick feeling of guilt settled in her stomach.

"I don't know, Shawn, maybe because I'm not a very good person."

"You need to stop playing games."

She nodded. When Shawn didn't deny her statement of character, it didn't go unnoticed by her. It stung a little, but she swallowed back her disappointment. She couldn't count on Shawn for everything. He wasn't just there to boost her ego and make her feel better about herself.

"And you should partner with Carson. He's a good header, and you're working toward the same goal... you two have so much drive, I'd hate to get in your way if you decided to team up."

"I'm not the only one who can make that decision."

"If you ask Carson, he'll probably say yes. He can't keep his eyes off you."

"That's called keeping an eye on the competition."

Shawn smiled. "I'm going to put Molly away. I'll meet you guys for food. And please, ditch the city boy."

"I'll do my best."

She watched Shawn walking away, and turned her attention back to Jack. It seemed strange that he was actually leaving her. Shawn was the guy that she thought would always be there, her safety net. But he was only human, and he could only take her games for so long. She'd taken advantage of his good nature, and now, her time was all used up. *Guess Chris was the final straw that broke the camel's back.*

"Looks like our winning run was by Tracy Miller and Shawn Dalton! For other standings, check the postings at the bottom of the announcer's stand."

A grin broke across her face, all thoughts of Shawn, Chris, and Carson faded away. She continued her journey toward the concessions where Carson and Chris were waiting.

Sure enough, she found them seated at a picnic table, each sitting at opposite sides and ends, putting as much distance between them as was physically possible. She shook her head and walked over, sitting in the middle of the bench that Carson was on.

"Congratulations," offered Carson.

"Thanks. I'm sure you finished high up there too."

"I'll have to check later."

"I've never seen anything quite like that. You made it look so easy," cut in Chris.

"Thanks. You must have been to a rodeo before, though. You live in Alberta."

"Rodeo isn't really my thing. But I like watching you."

"I can tell," muttered Carson.

Tracy stifled a laugh. This definitely wasn't Chris's comfort zone, and yet, he came out. *For her.* She felt a little guilty about wanting to send him away. He was a nice enough guy, and he made an effort, which was more than she could say for a lot of men.

Shawn walked up. "Coming to the after-party tonight?"

Tracy smiled. "You know me, I'll be there. Chris, you should join us."

None of the guys looked pleased at her invite, but Chris recovered the fastest. "Wherever you want to go is good enough for me."

Tracy smiled, but she noticed Carson rolling his eyes at Shawn. Well, the two of them could get over it, because it was her life, not theirs, and she could invite whomever she wanted. It wasn't like it was a private party.

CHAPTER ELEVEN

Carson sipped on his beer, not at all thrilled over how his day was going. He finished in third place, which meant he earned a few points, but he needed to be in first. And to top it all off, Shawn resigned as his partner. To say he was a little grouchy would have been putting it mildly. He was downright annoyed.

"Look man, it's not a big deal. If I back out, that frees you and Tracy up to be a team."

"I don't want to be on a team with her."

"I'm going to tell you what I told her," said Shawn, pausing to take a sip of his beer. "You two are putting way too much energy into competing with each other. If you directed that into working together and winning, nothing could stand in your way."

Carson shrugged. "She's… not someone I can handle."

"No one can. Don't try to harness her, just work *with* her."

"I'll think about it."

* * *

Tracy let Chris open the bar door for her. She glanced around, seeing a lot of familiar faces, but no sign of Carson and Shawn yet. She waved to a few people and nodded several greetings, but followed Chris through the crowded bar to a booth on the far side, away from the hub of the activity.

He remained a perfect gentleman all evening. Opening doors, taking her jacket, everything she wanted from a date, except that she never promised him a date. They were supposed to be here for drinks with friends, and instead, he guided her to a secluded booth and turned it into exactly what she wanted to avoid.

"Here're some menus," said a server, dropping them in front of Chris and her. "Can I start you off with anything to drink?"

"What's your special tonight?" asked Chris before Tracy could even get a word in edgewise.

"Four dollar domestic pints."

"We'll take two pints."

Tracy frowned. Did he just order for her? "Um, actually, I'd like a whiskey and Sprite, please."

The server smiled, nodding. "And what kind of beer would you like?" she asked Chris.

He looked annoyed. "Canadian is fine."

She took off to get their drinks and Tracy picked up her menu. She read over the items, using it as her chance to cool off a bit before she spoke to him again. She hated when men tried to control her, it was the biggest turnoff there could possibly be. Most other things were forgivable, but to act as if she didn't have an opinion, or a voice…

Calm down; he didn't mean any harm, she told herself.

"You're mad."

She didn't look up, but shrugged.

"What did I do wrong? Was it the drink? 'Cause I didn't mean anything by it."

"I know." She offered him a smile, this time, looking up. "Just bugged me a little, is all. I'm more than capable of making my own selections."

"Of course you are. I never presumed otherwise. I wasn't indicating that you couldn't, I just thought maybe you'd enjoy a night off from making any decisions."

Like he's doing me a favor? "Well, I don't. I like to be in control. The sooner you figure that out, the better."

She thought she saw a flash of annoyance cross his face, but it disappeared so fast, she thought she probably imagined it.

Their drinks came a moment later. "Are you ready to order?"

"Yeah, I'll have your chicken burger with a side of poutine."

Chris looked up, smiling at the waitress, but Tracy noticed his eyes weren't on her face. No, his eyes were fastened on her ample breasts. "How's your steak?"

"I like it."

"Good enough for me." His eyes rose to meet her face this time, and he smiled that charming smile that somehow managed to convince Tracy he was worth her time.

"Coming right up."

The waitress leaned over the table a little lower and further than necessary to gather up the menus, giving both Tracy and Chris a good look at her chest before standing up and walking off. Her hips swayed from side-to-side in her too-tight jeans, and Tracy looked over at Chris to find his gaze firmly glued to the waitress's backside. Rolling her eyes, she took a sip of her drink.

Chris returned his attention to her, offering a smile, but somehow, it seemed less friendly than before. She looked for something to talk about, something to break the silence while keeping things neutral. The only thing she could think of saying was to call him out for checking out their waitress. And confrontation was the last thing she wanted with a guy she hoped would be driving out of her life tonight.

"How's work?" she asked, finally unable to take the silence and choosing the safest topic she could think of.

"I don't want to talk about my work, and neither do you. Tell me about your partner."

She frowned. "My partner?"

"Yeah, the guy you were roping with. You two seemed pretty close."

She raised her eyebrows, taking another sip. "Are you seriously asking me about another guy right now?"

"Just trying to get the lay of the land," he replied with a smile that seemed less than sincere. His eyes flashed with what appeared to be jealousy.

"Shawn is an old friend. We grew up together."

"But nothing more?"

"Nothing on my part anyway."

He nodded slowly. "But on his part, there's something?"

"Yeah… wishful thinking."

"And the other one? The tall one?"

"Carson?" she let out a laugh. "He's my competition; he's the enemy."

"Ballads have been written about love between rivals."

She snorted, shaking her head. How could he actually think there was something between Carson and her? She could barely stand him before last night.

"Look, this is our first time hanging out," she said, purposely avoiding the word *date*. "I don't really think it's the appropriate setting to grill me on who I may or may not be interested in. I'm just looking to have a good time."

"Good, so am I."

She smiled, but it was forced. Something about the way he said that made her uneasy. And the way he looked at her made her wish she'd kept her jacket on.

"I, uh, I'm surprised you actually came out."

"I wasn't about to turn down a date with someone as beautiful as you."

She looked down, and the heat began rising in her face. Goosebumps formed on her arms that had nothing to do with the temperature. "You flatter me."

"I mean it. You're the entire package, Tracy: sexy, gorgeous, strong, and successful."

"I got kicked out of the professional rodeo circuit. Some might call that a failure."

"But you're fighting to get back in."

She lowered her eyes, not liking where the conversation was going. Chris was making it too personal and too focused on her.

"Oh, look, here's the food," she said, changing the subject as the waitress walked up.

Movement caught the corner of her eye and she saw Carson and Shawn walking in. Relief washed over her and she sat up taller in her seat, trying to get their attention as they looked around the packed bar for a table. Shawn's gaze focused in her direction and she waved him over.

* * *

Shawn nudged Carson and pointed over to a booth in the far corner where Tracy and Chris sat. He nodded, following his friend through the bar.

"Mind if we join you?" asked Shawn as they stood at the end of the booth.

Tracy shrugged, trying to appear indifferent, but she couldn't hide the visible relief on her face. She moved over, making room on the bench for Carson to join her. Chris did the same, letting Shawn in, but his face twisted into a sour look of annoyance.

"How's the food here?" asked Shawn.

"Not bad. The chicken burger is good. The waitresses are even better, just ask Chris," replied Tracy.

Chris's eyes flashed in anger over the obvious jab at him, but a subsequent smile seemed like an obvious effort to cover his true feelings.

The waitress approached their table a few minutes later. "Can I get you boys anything?" she asked.

Carson and Shawn placed their orders for food and drinks, and a couple minutes later, they were all sipping on beer. Tracy switched from her mixed drink to a pint.

Carson glanced from person-to-person. No one looked happy to be here. Shawn sat stiffly in the booth, on the very edge of the bench, putting as much distance between Chris and him as possible. Tracy couldn't meet Chris's eyes, so she stared at her drink, running her hands up and down the sweating glass, and erasing the fog.

"Tracy!"

Her head shot toward the bar where the voice came from and she waved.

"Hey, can you let me out?" she asked, pushing against Carson, who stood up before letting her out of the confining booth.

"Tracy Miller! That run today, you give us guys a run for our money," the cowboy boomed.

She flipped her braid over her shoulder and laughed. "Tony! Hey, I didn't even know you were here! Did you compete?" Her voice melded with the others filling the room as she walked over to the bar. Carson watched her. She threw her arm around the cowboy who called her over, and tilted her head back, laughing.

"Man, she's gorgeous," said Chris.

Carson looked over to see him watching her as well.

"You know what they say about the gorgeous ones?" he asked.

"They make one man very lucky?"

"They're the most dangerous," warned Carson.

Chris chuckled. "I'm not too worried about that. I'm not in it for the long-haul anyway."

What? He looked over at Shawn, who glared at Chris, but the guy didn't seem to notice. He must have been more than stupid to admit he just intended on using Tracy and discarding her as soon as he got sick of her.

"But you know what I mean. You guys have both had your time with her."

"Excuse me?" Shawn ground out through clenched teeth.

"You know, gotten to know her."

"Yeah, I've gotten to know her. But I sure as hell didn't discard her." He slid out of the booth, leaving his half-finished beer and walking away.

"You're an idiot, you know that?"

Chris shrugged, leaning back in the bench as if he didn't just make the biggest fool of himself. "What? The tension between you two tells me that whatever happened didn't end well."

"Yeah, we're competing for the same points. This isn't just a hobby, you know, it's a lifestyle. There is going to be tension."

Tracy walked over, a bounce in her step, and slid in beside Chris. She looked happier than when she left, and more comfortable. Chris slung his arm over her shoulder and it didn't even seem to faze her, but Carson's insides twisted at the sight.

"Sorry about that, some old friends."

"No problem. I have no issue with you hanging out with your friends."

She looked taken aback. Was it because he enjoyed her being a social butterfly? Or because he thought he needed to give her permission?

"Guess you can't complain too much, since I came with you," she said, hesitating over her words.

"And leaving with me." He winked.

Tracy smiled, but Carson couldn't help thinking she looked a little uncomfortable at the prospect. The images that leapt to mind definitely had him feeling uncomfortable. Actually, he was downright nauseated.

Shawn chose that moment to walk over, but instead of taking a seat, he put his hand on Tracy's shoulder and whispered in her ear. She nodded and got up.

"I'll be right back, guys. Don't get into any trouble while I'm gone."

Chris sipped his beer, but it was obvious he was trying to hide his annoyance at Shawn through the action. He knew his game was up. Shawn cared about Tracy too much to let her get used by some guy who waltzed into town, thinking he was a gift to women, and just because of… what? He was somewhat good looking? And a doctor? It might work on some girls, but Carson desperately hoped Tracy had enough self-respect to see straight through him.

He looked over his shoulder and saw Shawn and Tracy talking. Just by the way she shook her head, he could tell she wasn't impressed by what she was hearing. He just hoped she believed what Shawn had to say, and didn't chalk it up to *just* jealousy.

A short while later, Tracy came back. She practically stomped, and the loud clomping of her cowboy boots cut through the bar noise. She grabbed her coat, jamming her arms into each sleeve.

"I'm heading out. You staying here, at the motel?" she asked Chris.

He frowned. "Yeah. Can I give you a ride back? I picked you up, after all."

"I'll walk. Thanks, though."

He got up, following her to the bar to pay their tab. Carson watched, a silent observer, sipping the rest of his drink. Digging his wallet out of his pocket, he dropped a twenty on the table to cover his food and pint, and got up while Tracy and Chris were still busy with the cashier. She did a good job of remaining calm and amicable to Chris, but anyone could see that she was upset. And there was Chris, laying on the charm, trying to rectify what he screwed up. That would teach him to flap his big mouth around.

Stepping outside into the muggy, summer air, he donned his hat and leaned against the wall, waiting. It would rain soon. Tonight, maybe tomorrow; the air didn't get heavy like this without imminent rain. Good, the ground was too dry, too dusty. His dad had been praying for the clouds to open up all spring.

The doors burst open and Tracy walked out with Chris still in tow.

"Tracy, you know I wouldn't have said that. He's just jealous. Anyone with eyes can see that he's carrying a torch for you."

"Yeah, I know that. But he's also a friend, a friend that I trust, and he would never lie to me. What do I know about you?"

He reached for her, touching her shoulder, and she spun around. Carson half expected her to let her fist fly, but it remained clenched at her side.

"We had a great time tonight, I thought. I would really love to see where this is going."

"Not to your room, that's where."

"That's fine. I wasn't expecting that."

Liar. He frowned as he watched the dispute heat up. Tracy was no fool. No way would Chris get anywhere with her now.

Chris's shoulders fell, defeated. "Look, let me give you a ride back. No expectations."

"No, I'm fine."

"Call me tomorrow?"

She shrugged. "Don't hold your breath."

Chris turned away, walking back toward the bar. *Yeah, go drink away your disappointment. Who knows, maybe you'll snag a buckle bunny.*

Carson pulled his hat lower over his face, hoping Chris wouldn't notice him in the shadows as he re-entered the bar. As soon as the door closed, he trotted over to his truck and turned the key in the ignition. The engine rumbled to life and he maneuvered the beast of a truck through the cramped parking lot before turning right onto the main street. He could see Tracy walking just ahead. He crawled the truck forward and rolled down the window.

"Need a lift?" he asked.

She looked over, her face lit up by a streetlight, and her cheeks shining a little. Was she crying? He would have never guessed her to be a crier, but he was pretty sure that was what she was doing right now. She sniffled and nodded. "That'd be nice."

He stopped, put the truck in park and leaned over to open the door from the inside. She climbed in, plopping down in the seat and slouching.

Carson started to drive, but kept glancing over at Tracy. Her sniffles broke the silence every few seconds, and he could see her wiping away tears in his peripheral vision. He couldn't just take her back to her trailer like this. A crying girl inevitably grabbed a hold of his heart, and he knew he wouldn't be able to rest easy until she smiled again.

Driving into the rodeo grounds, he drove up to the stands instead of the trailers, and put the truck in park.

"What are you doing?" asked Tracy, wiping her eyes and looking up at where they were.

"I'm not letting you go back to your trailer like this. You need to talk?"

She shook her head. "Nope." She opened the door and jumped out, starting to walk in the direction of the trailers.

Carson jumped out after her, trotting to catch up. "You just can't make this easy, can you?"

"What? I don't know what this has to do with you."

"You're upset. I just want to help."

"You can't."

"Fine, then humor me."

She stopped, and he walked around to face her.

"With what?"

"Come with me. You don't have to talk if you don't want to. I just don't want to leave you upset. Okay? You'll be doing me a favor. I'll sleep better if you do."

She sighed, and then nodded. "Fine."

He wasn't really sure what he was doing, but he walked in the direction of the arena, looking over his shoulder to be sure she followed him. She did. Slowly, but she did. He opened the gate and it squealed on rusty hinges, echoing in the silence of the night.

"Ladies first."

"The sooner you learn that I'm not a lady, the better," she said, walking through.

"Maybe not a lady, but you're definitely a woman," he countered, watching her walk into the sand, her hips swaying as she stepped through the uneven terrain. He left the gate open, trotting after her and slinging his arm over her shoulder. He directed her to the middle, and then stopped.

"Here, this is my favorite place in the whole world."

Tracy turned around. "The middle of the Coalhurst arena?"

He kicked the toe of his boot in the sand a few times. "No, the middle of a rodeo arena. Doesn't matter what small town or big city it belongs to. The middle of an arena is where everything goes down, you know? It's where everything in life rights itself."

He looked at her for some kind of reaction. She slowly nodded and let her legs collapse under her, sitting cross-legged in the sand and running her hands over the grated surface.

"Why are you trying to do the impossible?" she asked, looking up at him with wide eyes. Her tears had all dried up, but even in the darkness, he could tell that her eyes were puffy from crying.

"Because it's my last chance to chase a dream. Why aren't you giving up on yours?"

"Because I don't know who I am without rodeo."

Carson pressed his lips together. That was a confession he was *sure* not many people ever heard. Tracy didn't exactly give the impression of someone lacking self-confidence. She walked around like she owned the world, and that was part of her allure. It was what drew Carson to her in the first place.

"Shawn thinks we should team up," she said.

"I know."

"I don't think he's wrong. I watched you rope; you're good. A little rusty, but good."

He snorted, sitting down beside her. "I'm good, eh?"

"Yeah. Not as good as me, but not many are."

"I'd ride with you, if you'll have me. And if you promise not to punch me."

"No promises."

"Can you warn me at least before letting any fists fly?"

"That I can do."

He rubbed the heel of his boot back and forth in the sand, digging a trench. He didn't know where to go from here. They'd made up, if that's what you could call it. It wasn't as if they'd ever been truly fighting, just at odds with each other. But now they just sat, quiet, nothing to say. And what he really wanted to ask was probably so personal it would end up with her storming off.

"I should have told you."

"What?"

"I should have told you about Chris. I wasn't going to."

Tracy shrugged. "You would have if Shawn hadn't. You wouldn't have let me go to his room."

"You don't know that. I hate getting involved in people's personal lives."

Tracy smiled and rested her head on his shoulder. How much did she have to drink? They hadn't been there that long, and he'd only seen her drink two. Was this just Tracy with her guard down? Open and inviting. She was a lot softer than he ever would have guessed.

"You're a decent guy. I knew that from the moment I met you."

"Thanks."

"I should have seen through him, though. I had my suspicions."

"Can I ask you something really personal?"

"You can ask, but I may not answer."

"But you won't storm off?"

Her head lifted off his shoulder and she gave him a lopsided smile. "Nah, I'm not really in the storming mood."

"Why did he upset you so much? It's not like you have a lack of men chasing after you."

Her face fell, and sadness filled her eyes. She looked down, digging her fingers into the sand and pulling up a fistful, before letting it run through her fingers. For a minute, he thought she wouldn't answer. Then she sighed.

"Because it's a scene that I'm all too familiar with."

"You're not the type of woman men *dare* to take advantage of."

"No, I'm not. But I've gotten a reputation around Coaldale as the fastest girl in town."

"A little Miranda Lambert isn't such a bad thing," he said, referencing a song.

She playfully punched him in the shoulder, and he pulled away, grinning. It was as if a barrier was finally broken between them. In the span of what, two weeks? They'd gone through attraction, to hatred, to friends. At least, that's what it felt like.

"Ow!"

"You know that's not what I meant."

"I can tell you aren't easy. And I went home with you before, so I would know."

"I'm not. But when you kiss a lot of boys, people just assume there's more going on."

"And you never bothered to correct anyone?"

"What's the point? They wouldn't believe me. Besides, it never really mattered to me. I was okay with what people whispered about me behind my back, because I made it out of that small town and into the big leagues."

"But when you got kicked out and stuck back at home, it only contributed to your identity as a failure."

"Yeah, something like that."

Carson looked at his boot. He felt like he should be divulging some kind of secret to her after she opened up to him, but he didn't know what would be appropriate to the situation, so he remained silent.

Tracy jumped to her feet. "Come on!"

He looked up, frowning. "Where?"

"I need to move."

She laughed and took off running across the expanse of the arena, sand flying up behind her boots, her arms outstretched like she was flying. Her laughter floated on the stale, stagnant air, waking up the night and Carson's heart. It pounded as he watched her play. She ran back and reached down, grabbing his hand. "Come on! Run with me!"

"I'm good here."

"Come on, Carson! I humored you. Now it's your turn to reciprocate and please me."

He got up slowly, a smirk lighting up his face, promising trouble where she couldn't hope to control it. "Please you? Oh, honey, I could please you in so many ways."

She rolled her eyes and started walking away from him backwards. "You wish."

"Is that a challenge?"

She shook her head, pressing her lips together as she restrained a smile, her braid flinging from side-to-side.

"I think I should prove you wrong."

He took off running and she screamed, turning and fleeing from him. He laughed, chasing her down and wrapping his arms around her torso, dropping them both into the sand in a heap. She rolled over in his arms, facing him, her chest rapidly rising and falling. Their faces were right up against each other, her nose touching his.

"This is dangerous," he breathed out in a whisper, knowing he should move, but lacking the will power to do so. Memories of her lips on his had his heart pounding in anticipation for what he knew could come next.

"I like danger."

That was all the encouragement he needed. He pressed his lips to hers, hungry for her taste. She responded in kind, and their mouths moved together, speaking louder than any words could. This was why they'd been fighting since they met; because she wanted him as badly as he wanted her, and neither knew what to do with those raw feelings.

Pulling back, he rolled off her and onto his back, putting some distance between them and allowing him to breathe some fresh air. He needed to get his wits about him before things went further than either one wanted.

His breathing grew labored, as if he'd just run a race instead of kissing the most beautiful, yet infuriating woman he'd ever met.

"Is that all you got, cowboy?" she asked, sitting up, and letting her braid fall over her left shoulder.

He nodded. "I don't want to do anything we might regret, Tracy."

She smiled, and stood up, offering her hand. He looked up at her and accepted it, clambering to his feet. She let go of him as soon as he stood and they started walking toward the gate he'd left hanging open.

He fell into step with her and they walked in silence. At the gate, she continued on, climbing into his truck while he latched it up.

It was a short jaunt to their trailers, and the time passed in complete silence. He parked in front of his trailer and turned off the ignition.

"Thanks," she said, opening her door.

"For what?"

"For turning my night around. I haven't laughed like that in a long time."

"That was all you." He reached forward, brushing a chunk of hair that fell out from her braid behind her ear.

"I know. But you got me there. If it weren't for you, I'd be moping in my trailer, nursing a beer, and wondering how I let my life get so messed up."

"Do you want me to walk you to your trailer?"

She shook her head. "I should be good from here. Besides, if anyone tries to mug me, I'm pretty sure I could kick his ass."

"I hear you have one hell of a right hook."

"Probably not anymore." She lifted her hand, devoid of any brace. "It's still pretty tender."

"But your left hand can probably pack a pretty mean punch, too."

"Good night, Carson."

"'Night."

She climbed out, slamming the truck door behind her, and disappearing into the dark. He sighed, leaning his head backwards, staring up at the ceiling of his truck. That woman had a way of turning him inside out and upside down.

Don't get too attached. She had an emotional night. Things will probably be back to normal in the morning. But he really hoped they weren't. Everything in him hoped they finally turned a corner in their relationship, or friendship, or whatever it was.

CHAPTER TWELVE

Tracy walked through the concessions and the stands. Each step of the designated "stairs" seemed too close together, but just a little too far apart to stretch out and take them two at a time. She settled for taking them one at a time and found a spot in the very top row near the edge, her favorite place to watch from. Opening her travel mug of coffee, she took a long sip. It was already her second cup of the day, but after the emotional roller coaster she'd been on last night, sleep hadn't come easy.

There isn't enough coffee in the world to get me through this day, she thought, rubbing her eyes with the heel of her left hand.

The morning events tended to be pretty tame on Sunday. A lot of kids' events. The more interesting stuff, like steer wrestling, was scheduled after lunch. But Tracy always enjoyed watching the kids trying to ride sheep, or scrambling for pigs. It brought back great memories of her introduction to the rodeo. How many of these kids would go on to build their careers in the rodeo? How many would line their shelves with all the buckles they won?

"Can I sit with you?"

Tracy didn't have to look to know Shawn was standing there. She nodded, watching the tractor run through the arena with the grater.

"I'm sorry about last night."

"Nothing to be sorry about. If anything, I should be thanking you for warning me about him."

"I shouldn't have just left you there."

Of course, Shawn would still be thinking of her. He always did. Why couldn't she care about him the way he did about her? She couldn't ask for anyone better. And yet, when she saw him, she saw only a friend, and never anything more than that.

"I chased you away. Don't worry about it."

"You didn't..." he trailed off.

"Go to his room anyway? No."

"Good."

She took another sip of her coffee. "Are you heading back to Coaldale today?"

"Yep. I'm hitched and ready to go. Just wanted to come see you before I left."

"I took your advice. I'm teaming up with Carson."

"I heard. I think you two will work well together." His words sounded pained and forced; and when she looked over at him, she saw a yearning in his eyes. He was letting her go; but that didn't make it any easier.

"If I don't break his nose."

That brought a smile to Shawn's face, but Tracy's mind drifted back to the night before, and the kiss she shared with Carson. It was one for the books, that's for sure. She never had a kiss make her heart race like that. That man could bring out myriad of emotions in her—anger being only one of them.

"He's fast on his feet. He won't let a swing connect."

She smiled, nodding her agreement. He did have an uncanny way of knowing what was going through her head.

She angled her legs toward Shawn and leaned forward, hugging him. "Drive safe, okay? And don't be a stranger."

"I should be telling you that."

"I'll be on the road for a while, so it'll be up to you to come see me."

"And after?"

She shrugged. "Anywhere but Coaldale."

Hurt flashed in his eyes, but he nodded. He understood. She knew he would. He knew her reputation there, and why she had no desire to return.

"I'll stay close by, though. Don't you worry; I'm not exiting your life."

"I wouldn't let you."

He stood up, and walked down the awkward bleachers before disappearing into the growing crowd.

Tracy sighed, leaning back against the top of the bleacher. She hated seeing Shawn hurt, and really hated being the one who did that to him. Most of all, she hated how the whole time he sat there, she kept thinking about Carson and the way he made her head spin.

Various people waved to her, or stopped to chat throughout the morning. In the rodeo circle, people knew her. She always made a point of riding in these small-town rodeos—they kept her busy and provided practice between the professional rodeos. She'd ridden with a lot of these people before making the pro circuit.

Funny thing was, not a single pro rider said anything to her. There were only a couple, but they seemed to deliberately avoid her. And the people here, the regulars, the ones who had fun, still treated her as a friend. Nothing changed. No one cared if she were amateur or pro, they just enjoyed spending time with her.

"Goes to show who my true friends are," she mumbled.

"Talking to yourself is a sign of insanity."

That voice, quiet and shy, yet masculine and strong at the same time, made her breath hitch in her throat while butterflies performed acrobatics in her stomach. She looked up and met Carson's deep brown eyes.

"Morning, cowboy."

"Sleep well?" he asked, folding his tall frame to sit next to her.

"Not so great. You?"

"Like a baby."

Tracy frowned. She hated that saying. "By that, do you mean that you slept soundly, or were you up every couple of hours?"

Carson laughed. "Soundly."

"See? That saying makes absolutely no sense to me."

"It's too early to get into it. I haven't even finished my coffee yet."

They sat in silence. A comfortable silence. The kind that she used to enjoy with her dad. There weren't many other people she could savor it with. Apparently, Carson joined the ranks and brought the list up to a nice, even two.

Kids wearing hockey helmets streamed into the arena and lined up. The announcer explained the rules for the pig scramble—which weren't many.

The whistle blew, and the kids raced into the group of pigs, as the squeals of pigs and the laughter and shouts of kids filled the arena when the two groups met. Tracy couldn't help grinning, and Carson let out a chuckle beside her.

"Did you do the pig scramble as a kid?"

"I was the pig scramble queen," she replied.

"Of course you were. Is there anything you weren't good at?"

She shrugged. "I can't really steer wrestle. Not bulky enough."

That brought out a full-on guffaw from Carson. "I can almost see you trying, though."

"Oh, I did. I was sixteen and there was a branding in Foremost that my dad took me to. I was convinced that if scrawny, sixteen-year-old Shawn could dog the steers, so could I."

"What happened?"

"I got dragged around the pen."

He grimaced.

"I ate a lot of dirt and eventually got kicked off. The cowboys found it fairly entertaining."

"And that was the last time you tried?"

She smiled, shaking her head. "Nope. I went home and Shawn let me wrestle his dad's steers until I finally got one down. *That* was the last time I ever did it. I think every muscle in my body hurt for a month after that."

"I should have known."

"I also got into roping because everyone told me girls barrel raced and boys roped. I didn't much like hearing that."

Carson smiled, shaking his head, but saying nothing. His eyes said it all. To Tracy, they seemed to sparkle with admiration, and drew her in, until she had to repress the urge to kiss him.

She stood up, needing more distance between them. *Now.* "I'm going to go grab some breakfast. I'll see you later."

Carson nodded, turning his attention to the arena where the kids still raced after the pigs. They were quick little buggers.

* * *

Carson tried not to watch Tracy leave. But even though he kept his eyes on the kids and pigs in the arena, his mind replayed the events from last night. He wanted to kiss her so badly. But he didn't want to assume that what happened last night was anything more than them getting caught up in the moment. And since she didn't invite him to eat breakfast with her, he was starting to think there was probably a little bit of regret on her part. He didn't blame her. It would make their working relationship a lot harder if romance got mixed in.

It wasn't very fun to watch the morning events, but he didn't have much else to do. Pulling out his phone, he checked the display. No missed calls, no texts. His dad promised he would be here yesterday, but he hadn't seen or heard from him. Something must have come up.

Dialing his dad's number, he held the phone to his ear and listened to it ring.

"Carson, I'm sorry I didn't make it yesterday," his dad answered without even saying hello.

"It's okay, Dad. How are things at home?"

"Busy, as usual. But that's not why you called. How did it go yesterday?"

"I came in third." The words left a bitter taste on his tongue. Every time he imagined calling his dad from the rodeo, it was to say he won, not that he came in third.

"Not bad."

"Not good enough."

His dad sighed. "There's always the farm. You could just let go of this pipedream and come back."

Carson ignored his dad's suggestion. The word *farm* just sounded like a prison sentence to him, and he'd already served more time than he wanted to. "Are you going to come out at all? I'm going to be in Claresholm next weekend."

"I'll try. But no promises, though. The farm comes first."

The farm *always* came first, which was why he was a little shocked when his dad promised to come and watch him, and also why he wasn't surprised when he didn't show. That was just life, and he was more than familiar with it.

"Okay. Well, I'll call you when I get there."

Hanging up, he stood and slipped his phone into his back pocket before making his way down the bleachers. He didn't know many people around here, Shawn was probably already gone, and that left only Tracy. Maybe she wouldn't be opposed to his company—and she could introduce him to some people later. If he wanted to run in these circles, he needed to make some more friends.

Walking to her trailer, the sound of banging met his ears. *Who could be making a racket like that?* He frowned.

"I know you're in there. I just want to talk."

The voice was all too familiar. He strode around the corner, and sure enough, a man with a mop of blond hair stood in front of Tracy's trailer, his fist slamming against her door. Rage rose inside Carson, and before he could even think about what he was doing, he covered the distance between them and clamped his hand on Chris's shoulder, spinning him around to face him.

"Hey, man, what's your problem?"

"Leave. Her. Alone!" he ordered, squeezing his shoulder.

Chris jerked backwards, out of his grasp, his eyes blazing. "This is none of your business. This is strictly between Tracy and me."

"You made it my business the minute you told me you intended to use her. Just admit that you're done here, and leave while you still have some dignity left."

The smile that crossed the man's lips could only be described as cocky. It wasn't quite a smile, maybe closer to a leer. Either way, it had Carson's blood instantly boiling.

"You gonna call security on me?"

He laughed. "Security? No, I wouldn't give them the pleasure of escorting you out. I'll take you out myself."

Chris seemed to be studying him, looking him up and down, deciding whether or not it was worth the fight. Carson flexed his muscles a bit. Not in an obvious way, but taut enough that they were visible, about a warning not to pick a fight.

"Fine, I'm outta here. You guys are all crazy anyway."

"Yeah, I'm the crazy one," he muttered, watching Chris stomp away. He practically threw a fit, kicking up dirt a few times. The guy was such a child, and obviously not used to losing. Well, good riddance. No one needed him around, least of all, Tracy.

The door opened and Tracy stood there, looking a little pale, but standing tall and proud.

"He's gone, and I don't think he'll be coming back," Carson said.

"Thanks for that. You wanna come in for a minute?"

She stood back, allowing him in. He closed the door behind him and walked to the middle of the trailer. It looked different in the daylight. Not as sad. He could see the clutter of her life filling the small space she called her home. But that was the thing, it looked like a home: from the pile of western and horse magazines beside the recliner, to the dirty dishes in the sink, and homemade curtains to replace the ones that were factory-installed.

"You keep fighting my battles for me," she said, pouring a cup of steaming coffee. She handed it to him and he accepted it, sipping the burning liquid. It scalded his tongue, but gave him a reason to delay his response. He didn't want to say the wrong thing, to make her feel even more vulnerable than she already did.

"You could have handled it."

She shrugged, sitting down opposite him. "As long as he's gone for good, I don't care who handled him."

"Claresholm next?" he asked, changing the subject.

She nodded, already looking more relaxed now that the conversation was about business. "I say we head over there and make use of the rodeo grounds, unless you need to go home for a bit."

"Sounds good to me." He got up. "I'm gonna go pack up. I'll see you there?"

"Yeah, let's do supper and figure out our schedule for the summer."

"Thanks for the coffee."

He set the mug down on the counter and left her trailer; a place that was becoming all too familiar to him. And surprisingly, he didn't mind. Just walking away left him feeling a little emptier, and he fought the urge to turn around and go right back in. But he kept walking. There was plenty of time to get to know Tracy better.

She'll have to become all the more familiar over the next few months, he thought.

CHAPTER THIRTEEN

Tracy sat below the awning of her trailer and sipped a mug of coffee that was cooling faster than she was drinking it. Her mind spun over the events of the last twenty-four hours. She kept telling herself she didn't much like how Carson fought her battle today; but at the same time, she couldn't deny her relief over knowing he stood in her corner.

Only problem was: she couldn't get the memory of the kiss they shared last night out of her head. The scene kept replaying in her mind. Did she come on too strong? Had she ruined their partnership before it even began? She shook her head and drained the lukewarm coffee from the cup. Carson made no indication that the events of last night were starting something weird between them. Unlike the last time their lips met, this time, they seemed to be in a good place. They were both after the same thing, and needed to stay on the same page if either one hoped to achieve it.

Tracy just didn't know what page she wanted to be on. She liked Carson. That was why she kept talking to him, and dragging him back into her life, despite their disagreements, or temporary disdain for each other. Even though he was formerly her competition, she felt a magnetic pull toward him whenever he was near.

It was only an hour's drive to Claresholm, and nothing was keeping her here now that she collected her earnings. A shiny new buckle sat in the drawer in her trailer, among all the others. Rather than stay and continue letting her mind spin in confusion over Carson, she began packing her belongings. She threw the clothes that littered the tiny floor area around her bed into the cupboards, without bothering to fold or hang them, and put the dishes that sat in the drying rack in their respective places. Within fifteen minutes, the interior of her trailer looked tidy, if not downright clean.

Whenever she settled, even if it were only for a couple of nights, Tracy tended to *really* settle in. She wasn't exactly a domestic goddess when it came to maintaining the house. Spring and fall cleaning were about the extent of it, and those invariably took a good few days, despite the tiny trailer. Even now, sand and dirt littered the linoleum floor. Long ago, she ripped out all the carpet and replaced it with cheap vinyl to make cleaning faster and easier. A quick sweep was all it took and that too was taken care of.

An hour later, her truck and trailer pulled onto the highway, driving toward Claresholm. This rodeo was a small town again, and the stakes weren't high. She'd be seeing the same people from the last rodeo trickling into Claresholm over the week. She and Carson wouldn't have to share the rodeo grounds for the first couple of days.

Pulling into the parking area, she saw Carson's truck and trailer already there. Carson was in the arena, riding his horse and rehearsing patterns. He was a great rider, made apparent by the way he moved as one with the horse. He was well-trained, and he and his horse had a visible partnership, which was sorely needed in this business. His mount seemed eager to please, and did whatever his master asked of him. But Carson was also fluid, intuitively sensing his horse's movement and emotions, and responding accordingly.

They were poetry in motion. Tracy wondered if she looked like that when she rode. It certainly felt like poetry when she rode Jack, but she wasn't sure everyone else observed it, or to the extent she saw it in Carson.

Pulling up beside Carson's trailer, she parked her truck and unloaded Jack. She gave him a few minutes to settle in and drink some water while she paid her fees to the rodeo board.

She rifled through her trailer, finding the papers that indicated which stalls she reserved so she didn't have to track someone down.

I need to get more organized, she thought. *Maybe empty one of these cupboards and dedicate it only to my paperwork.*

Finding the information she needed, she hopped back outside where Jack patiently grazed at the back of the trailer, picking a few weeds and grass that poked through the gravel. She picked up his lead and walked toward the stalls. They sported a roof and sides, but the fronts were exposed, and the backs were shared with other stalls, typical rodeo setup.

"Here you go, boy. Home sweet home for another week."

At least these stalls closed a bit easier than the ones at Coalhurst. And by easier, Tracy still had to use both hands and some muscle, but at least she didn't have to throw her whole body into it.

Walking down to the grounds office, she entered without knocking.

"Hello?" she called out.

A short, somewhat plump woman walked out. She carried her weight well, though, and her hair was pulled up in a ponytail. Her jeans and button-up shirt were a flattering choice. "Can I help you?"

"Just here to pay my board and rodeo dues."

"Ah, yes, you're with the handsome young man that came in earlier, right?"

"Yep."

"All paid up."

Tracy frowned. "What? That can't be right."

"Two stalls for the week, a team roping entry, and two parked trailers, right?"

"Yeah," she said hesitantly. "But he was only supposed to pay for his half."

The woman shrugged. "Look, honey, I just accept payment. If I were you, I'd accept his gift with a smile. Maybe he just wanted to do something nice for you."

Tracy put on a smile, but inside, her stomach churned with discomfort. "Yeah, maybe. Thanks for your help."

She left the building and walked over to the arena where Carson brought his horse to a halt. He was in the middle of the arena and leaned over, patting the horse on the neck.

"Hey!" she called out, climbing over the fence and jumping down into the loose sand. The impact of her feet hitting the ground sent a spike of pain through her heels and up her legs, but she endured it without a grimace as she walked toward him.

He looked up and waved. Annoyance coursed through her, and she had to take deep breaths. *It's not a big deal, he meant no harm*, she kept thinking to herself, trying to level her temper. But she just couldn't shake her discomfort over him paying her fees.

"Hey, all settled in?"

"Yep, and then I went to pay up; imagine my surprise when she told me you already paid."

Carson grinned, and looked proud of himself, like he'd done her a favor or something. His expression fell a little when he saw what she hoped was a sardonic smile. *Good, let him squirm.*

"I feel like this is something that should have been discussed, instead of you just going ahead and doing it."

"I'm just trying to pull my own weight. This is a team, Tracy. That means we help each other out."

She stopped next to his horse and rested one hand on his neck. "Yeah, we split the costs. Like you pay your half and I pay mine. I don't need you looking after me, Carson. Okay? I don't need to feel like I owe you anything."

He scoffed, removing his hat and running a hand through his hair. "Is that what this is about? Me trying to look after you?"

"First, you give me a ride home, you make it your personal mission to cheer me up, then you send Crazy Chris packing, and now you're paying my fees...." she trailed off, her frown deepening. He laughed, actually *laughed*. Quietly, but still, he laughed. His shoulders shook, his eyes danced, and if he weren't laughing at her, his grin would have been infectious. In this case, however, it just caused her blood to boil even hotter.

"You think this is a joke?" she asked, keeping her voice calm.

His grin faded a little, but only because he appeared to be trying to stifle it, not because her words were actually getting through to him.

"No ma'am," he managed to squeak out just before a snicker.

She rolled her eyes and turned on her heel, stomping away.

"We still on for dinner?" he called after her.

She lifted her hand and a very specific finger pointed straight into the air. Yeah, they were still on for dinner, but she intended to let him stew on it for a bit. Maybe then he'd realize that for this to work, communication was key, like she was doing right now. She dropped her hand. It was hard to stay mad at him when he smiled. He had that guilty look in his eye, like he just stole the last cookie from the cookie jar; but he didn't need to know that.

* * *

Carson watched her walk away. Yep, he loved watching her walk through sand arenas; each step in the soft footing accentuating the movement of her hips. When she lifted her finger into the air, he wanted to yell out that she wasn't being very lady-like, but she said herself that she detested that adjective, and he really couldn't see her acting like one anyway. Her reaction was so... Tracy.

He half expected it. It wasn't like he was unaware that she didn't want to be looked after. It was his way of letting her know he wasn't trying to ride her coattails to go pro. He wanted this for the long haul. He planned to make it a career, and if they worked well together, he'd like to build his with her.

Sure, he could have let her pay her half, but he had more reasons for doing what he did than not. He wanted to do something nice for her after everything that happened with Chris, and seeing how upset she was last night. And then there was *the kiss*... the one that he couldn't get out of his mind. Paying was his way of conveying he was open to taking that kiss further, without saying it in words or engaging in an awkward conversation over it. And, personal reasons aside, Carson wanted to make it loud and clear that he was in the partnership one hundred percent.

He dismounted, leading Danny-boy out of the arena. They'd been working patterns and doing flatwork for the last hour, and his horse was good and sweaty. He wasn't in peak shape, like Carson would have preferred, but after a couple of weeks on the road, and living that life, he would be.

He removed Danny's tack and led him over to the watering station, giving him a quick rinse with the hose before returning him to his stall.

It had to be close to dinnertime, but Carson needed a shower. After a few days, he felt pretty sure he was ripe enough that he was starting to smell. At least, he caught a whiff of something offensive in his truck while driving up, and if he could smell himself, that could only mean everyone else would notice it too. Good thing everyone else at the rodeo was carrying a similar scent. *Haut au equis. Pleasant.*

Collecting a towel, he grabbed the backpack he kept his shampoo and razer in. He threw in a clean set of clothes, and went off to find a place to clean up.

There were some Port-a-Potties set up near the arena and stands, but no shower house. Maybe he could find a gym nearby, or a public pool. He decided to take a quick drive through town and see what was there.

Turning on his truck, a knock sounded on his window. *Tracy.* Rolling it down, he smiled. "Come to apologize?"

"Nope. Where you headed?"

"I need a shower. Know where I can find one?"

She tipped her head toward her trailer. "Just use mine."

He shrugged, opening the truck door. "Thanks. I wasn't really looking forward to begging for a shower like a homeless person."

She ushered him into the trailer. "Make yourself at home. I'm gonna feed Jack. Does Danny need anything?"

"Just a couple scoops of complete feed. It's in the front of my trailer."

"'Kay. Don't use up all the water, or you'll be filling the holding tank."

"Yes, ma'am," he saluted her, closing himself into the tiny bathroom that made up the space between the common living area and her bedroom. The door to her bedroom was open, allowing him a glimpse into her life. The bed was made, but things were strewn all across it. Cupboards hung open, revealing clothes stuffed inside, not a single item looked folded or cared for.

He sighed, closing that door as well. He had no right to snoop. She'd been kind enough to let him into her life, the least he could do was respect her privacy.

Starting the water, he got the temperature to the right point of hot to make his skin tingle, but not burn, and climbed into the plastic cubby that claimed to be a shower. He had to hunch over to get under the pathetic stream of water and quickly rinsed himself all over. He turned the water off while lathering the two-in-one shampoo and conditioner.

Rinsing off quickly, he dried off one leg, then stepped out and began toweling off the other in order to keep the puddle of water he was sure to leave on the floor at a minimum.

Dressing was a whole different challenge. The trailer was obviously not made for someone of his stature. He got his pants on, then balanced on one leg, trying to pull on his socks. He teetered and caught himself before trying again.

This is ridiculous, he thought. Setting his foot down, he got to work on the other sock, yanking it on as quickly as possible. He realized his mistake when he teetered to the left, and jumped reflexively, trying to regain his balance. The jumping only shook the trailer, thereby worsening his precarious situation. He closed his eyes, realizing what was happening, before bracing for the impact.

His shoulder hit the door first, and then it took a second before the rest of him landed on the floor. "Oomph!"

He lay still for a minute with his eyes closed, then opened them slowly. He knew he'd broken through the door; that much was apparent.

"I leave you alone for five minutes and you're already breaking my trailer?"

He cringed, seeing a set of cowboy boots only inches from his face. Sitting up painfully, he looked at Tracy with her hands on her hips, and one eyebrow arched higher than the other. Her look was rather ambiguous, and he couldn't quite decipher between amusement and disbelief. Perhaps it was both.

"Though really, how many girls could say they had a handsome, shirtless cowboy fall through their trailer door?"

He groaned, and closed his eyes before standing up, and brushing off the shoulder that took the brunt of the fall. He felt the heat rising up into his face. Calling the whole scene embarrassing would have been making light of the situation. He'd broken her door, was half naked, and there she stood, ogling him. Mortified was a better description for how Carson felt.

Inspecting the damage, he groaned again. "I am so sorry, Tracy. I'll fix this, I promise."

A hole, roughly the shape and size of his shoulder was neatly punched through the first layer of the hollow core door, and the latch appeared mangled beyond repair.

"Yeah, you will. But let me enjoy this fleeting moment first."

She continued to smile with her lips pressed together as if holding something back, and her eyes squinted in amusement.

Finally, a giggle escaped, which soon turned into a full laugh. She leaned against the kitchen counter, and doubled over, roaring with laughter.

Shaking his head, he retreated into the bathroom to get his shirt on. Reaching for the door, he tried to close it, but it crashed to the ground. He stood there looking bewildered, in the doorway to the bathroom, with the door lying on the ground. Tracy doubled over again; laughing so hard, she began hyperventilating.

"I'm glad you find this so amusing," he growled, grabbing his shirt off the toilet lid, and tossing his things into his backpack, before leaving. He almost slammed the trailer door behind him, but feared he'd break another door in Tracy's home. He stopped and latched it with care before storming off toward his truck.

He finished getting dressed, and ran a comb through his hair, then clamped his hat on his head.

A knock sounded on his trailer door before it opened. Tracy stood there, her long, curly hair down, for once, and looking every bit as wild as she was. It suited her.

"You should leave your hair down more often," Carson said, grabbing his wallet off the mattress and shoving it into his back pocket.

Her face took on a funny look, like she didn't know what to make of his compliment. "Uh, thanks. Ready to go?"

"Yep."

He stepped down, closing the door. Since his truck was already unhooked from the trailer, they climbed in there.

"Where to?" he asked, turning the key in the ignition.

She shrugged. "Let's just drive and see where it takes us."

So much about those words made him uncomfortable, and he couldn't help thinking she wasn't just talking about dinner. "Can we find out what's around before we start driving? For all we know, we might have to drive to the next town over."

"You like having a plan, don't you?" she asked, frowning as she studied him.

Plan? Sure, if not jumping blindly into things means I like having a plan. Carson didn't see himself as uptight, but rather flexible. He just liked to have a general idea.

"What's wrong with having a plan?"

"Nothing. It just takes all the adventure out of life."

He put the truck into drive, pulling out of the rodeo grounds. Fine, she wanted adventure, he'd do things her way.

Driving down Main Street, they saw the motel and bar, and what looked to be a generic family restaurant, but the lights were out and it seemed deserted—likely closed for the day. On the outskirts lay an old, barn-like building that was lit up with tiny, white Christmas lights, but it didn't look tacky, not like the owners were just too lazy to take them down. No, it gave the place a charm, and looked like starlight. Big bay windows on the sides of the barn revealed candles in each window, shimmering and lit despite the daylight outside.

Without a word, he pulled in and parked.

The parking lot was fairly empty still. But in a small town, how much business could happen on a Sunday?

He was actually surprised to find it open. A lot of these types of places were closed on Sundays. Many small towns shut down completely. And Claresholm looked pretty dead.

"This looks nice," said Tracy. "Aren't you glad we decided to embark on an adventure?"

"I'll give you an answer once we've tasted the food."

He climbed out and made his way around the truck to open her door, but she already jumped out and slammed the door behind her.

"M'lady?" he asked, offering her his arm.

Tracy looked, and raised her eyebrow. "I'm no lady, cowboy."

She walked past him, grabbing the huge wooden door of the restaurant and pulling it open. Rather than holding it open for him, however, she walked right on through. He jogged up, catching the door before it closed, and slipped inside.

That was Carson's kind of door. Heavy, solid, firm... if he fell into that door, he'd have probably broken his shoulder rather than having his shoulder break the door.

They stood by the sign that requested they wait to be seated. He shuffled his feet, shoving his hands into his pockets. Tracy looked around and paced, before walking to the counter and hitting a service bell that sat there.

"Be right there, hon!" came a shout from the back.

She shrugged, looking at him. "Hope the food is good, cause the service, so far, is less than stellar."

"What happened to being laid back and going with the flow? It's Sunday night; cut the woman some slack."

A second later, the woman walked around from the kitchen, wiping her hands on her black apron that looked quite stuffed full of change, multiple pens, and a pad of paper. "Table for two?" she asked, giving them a tired smile.

The woman was stunning, and not at all what Carson pictured after she called Tracy "hon." No, he envisioned a short, plump, grandmotherly type; and this woman was anything *but* that. She was petite, and on the shorter side, but slim. Her long, brown hair was pulled back into a ponytail. She wore those tight jeans that you had to wear inside your boots, instead of outside, and a pair of white cowboy boots. Her shirt was a plain, white blouse.

"Yeah, for two," replied Tracy, jabbing him in the ribs.

He was staring and didn't even realize it.

"Right this way."

She led them through the empty restaurant to a table near the back. It was situated in the middle of a bay window that looked out to rolling hills. The building was definitely a refurbished barn. It had a half loft, that was open on their side, giving that half of the restaurant a huge, vaulted ceiling and grand view of the barn-roof.

"Can I get y'all anything to drink?" she asked as she set menus in front of them while they took their seats.

"MGD for me." Tracy sounded terse and short.

"I'll have the same, please."

"Coming right up."

Once they were alone, Tracy sighed, planting her elbows on the table and resting her chin on her hands.

"She's in Western Canada, not the Southern States. Don't know why she's going around saying 'hon' and 'y'all'. It sounds ridiculous."

Carson's eyes widened in surprise. Where was that coming from? The woman hadn't done anything but lead them to their table, and Tracy was ready to attack her. "Maybe she's from the States."

"Or maybe she thinks it's cute to talk like a Southern belle." Tracy adopted an exaggerated, Southern drawl and grinned, albeit maliciously.

They fell silent as the woman returned with their drinks.

"Ready to order?"

"Um, I need a few more minutes," he replied, realizing he hadn't even opened the menu.

"May I suggest the pork tenderloin? It's been slow-cooked on the smoker and it'll just melt in your mouth."

"Oh, it'll melt in your mouth. Doesn't that sound nice?" asked Tracy, her words rather sexually suggestive. She was definitely not commenting on the pork.

"Yeah, that sounds good. Thank you," he said, ignoring Tracy.

"And for you?" she turned to Tracy.

"I'll have the same."

Tracy took a swig of her beer and stared out the window. The restaurant was abandoned, and it was just the two of them and the staff.

"What's gotten into you, Tracy?"

"Nothing."

"Why are you attacking that poor woman?"

"I'm not; I'm merely making an observation."

Carson studied her. She refused to look at him while she spoke, and her answers were terse, sharp, and her tone biting.

"You're jealous!"

Her face turned crimson red, and she met his eyes, while hers flashed in anger. "I am not! What do I have to be jealous of?"

"You caught me looking at her and you're jealous. Come on, Tracy, I wasn't even checking her out. You know I'm not that kind of guy."

"Actually, I don't know that about you. We're business partners, nothing more."

"Tell that to the kiss we shared last night."

"It was just a kiss."

Carson studied her as she looked out the window, refusing to meet his eyes, and sipped her beer. Enough was enough. He couldn't handle all this tension if they were going to be partners. He got up, walking over to her.

"What are you doing?" she asked, looking up at him.

He leaned down, tangling his fingers in her hair, and kissed her. She immediately responded, pushing into his lips, asking for more than he was giving. He drew away, out of breath, and grinned.

"You were jealous," he said, feeling pretty smug as he returned to his seat.

"So what if I were?" she asked, staring down at her spoon like it was a specimen to be studied.

He reached forward, placing his hand on hers. "Tracy, I like you a lot. I think you like me too. The only reason I didn't make another move after last night was because I didn't know if it would be welcomed. But if you want to see where this goes as much as I do..." he trailed off.

"It's a bad idea. We're working together."

"And it's a better idea to keep our feelings all pent-up? So that I can get jealous of every guy that looks sideways at you? And you can make underhanded comments to every woman I look at?"

"Don't think that would change if we started dating."

He squeezed her hand. "At least, we'd be on the same page. What do you say? Can we call this our first date?"

She looked at him with wide eyes, and bit her lip, then slowly, oh-so-slowly, she nodded.

CHAPTER FOURTEEN

Carson sat opposite Tracy at the local bar in Coleman, celebrating their first place run with a couple of beers. Out of the last five rodeos, they placed in every one.

He picked at a basket of fries, lifting one out and looking at it. "We have a bit of a break now. Are you thinking about heading home for a bit?"

She sipped her beer, then shook her head. "I don't have any place to call home, and don't need one."

He cringed, bringing his bottle to his lips to conceal his reaction. He understood, he really did; the need to be on the road, feeling more at home surrounded by trucks, trailers, horses, and the smell of deep fried food from concession stands. But a part of him hoped she'd feel some kind of draw to family. As much as he loved the road, family and home were important to him; and had been for his whole life up until now.

"How would you feel about coming back to Foremost with me this week? Meeting my family?"

She looked up at him, eyes wide, and her hand halfway to her mouth with a fry clutched between her fingers.

"Uh, that's pretty... I mean," she stumbled over her words, obviously unsure of how to react, or maybe just scared of hurting him.

"Look, if you aren't comfortable with it, that's fine," he quickly back pedaled. It was too soon. They'd only been together for a little over a month. He felt a lot closer to her than a few short weeks, however. Living in such close quarters, even if they were in separate trailers, and working together, day in and day out, tended to put a relationship in fast forward. You skip past the honeymoon stage real fast, not that they ever really had that.

"No, it's okay. It might be nice to meet your parents."

"Really?" He wasn't expecting that, not after her initial reaction.

"Sure, it'll be good to get off the road."

"Oh, well, yeah. Okay. That's great. I'll give them a call and let them know we're coming."

He grabbed his phone off the table. Tracy grimaced and he paused, ready to dial the number. "What?"

"Just, maybe don't tell them I'm your girlfriend," she mumbled, her eyes downcast. She shoved a few fries in her mouth, obviously trying to create an excuse to stop the conversation.

Not tell them she was his girlfriend? It seemed strange, but at the same time, not. It was a big step, and maybe she wanted a trial run with his family without all the pressure of being tagged the *new girlfriend*. He could understand that. He just didn't like it. He wanted to show her off, and brag that *he* snagged a girl like her. Because, anyone had to admit, she was incredible; strong, capable, and a talented roper and rider. Tracy Miller was the complete package to him. *But not the ideal farmer's wife*, his mind chided. He ignored that thought and pressed send on his parents' number. It didn't matter if she weren't farmer's wife material. He didn't plan on being a farmer.

"Hello?"

"Hey, Mom, it's Carson."

"Carson! How're you doing? We've been following your points online. Looks like you've been doing really well too.

You're getting close to applying for the pros, right?" She kept going, barely taking a breath.

Carson chuckled. "I'm doing pretty good, Mom. But look, the reason I'm calling is to tell you we have a bit of a break between rodeos this week, and we'd like to come home for a visit."

"*We?*" she asked, putting an emphasis on the fact that he wouldn't be coming alone. Of course, she would pick up on that.

"Yeah, Mom, *we*. Tracy and I. You know, my roping partner."

"Oh, Tracy, I see. I didn't realize you were roping with a girl. Your dad said you partnered up with a Josh, or was it Justin?"

"Shawn. Yeah, for one rodeo, and he went back home."

"Well, nice that you could find another partner so fast. So, when do you think you'll be back here?"

"Around lunchtime tomorrow."

"I'll have food waiting. We just can't wait for you to be back home! We want to hear all about how things have been going this past month."

"I can't wait to tell you all about it. I'll see you tomorrow, Mom."

He smiled, hanging up. She was probably still talking. That woman, his mother, loved to chat. So opposite his dad, who was the strong, silent type. Carson must have inherited that from him. How he cared for others, and couldn't turn it off, however, that was all from his mom.

"My mom is really excited," he said, shoving a fry in his mouth.

"Sounds like it."

"You don't seem to be."

Tracy shrugged.

"Are you scared? Tracy Miller is scared?"

"I'm not scared. I'm just not overly excited."

He smirked. He didn't believe her. She was scared; shaking in her boots, meet the parents, scared. He never would have guessed he'd see the day. But she was doing her best to hide it.

"It'll be fine. They'll love you, especially since you *aren't* my girlfriend."

"But I'm taking you away from the farm."

"The farm lost me long before I hit the road with you. It's not like you rolled up and enticed me to want this life. I was already here when you came into my life."

He reached over the table and took her hand, rubbing his thumb across it. She didn't have soft hands like most women. No, Tracy's were muscled and calloused. Her fingers and palms were rough, like sandpaper, from hours upon hours of gripping ropes and reins. Some men might have found it unattractive, or unfeminine, but he thought it completed her. If he touched her hand and it was soft, it just wouldn't have been Tracy.

"You'll wow them, like you wow me every single day. Now, let me buy you another drink. We had a big win today."

Tracy grinned, nodding. "I never say no to a cold beer."

* * *

Being with Carson was… hard, a lot harder than she expected. Sure, the attraction was undeniably there, and it was still healthy and strong. But she was opinionated, and despite his shyer nature, Carson wasn't afraid to stand up to her. It was both frustrating and liberating at once.

She climbed into bed that night, staring up at the ceiling of her trailer, and thinking about the weekend. Coleman was their last rodeo until the second weekend of May. They'd have a longer road trip ahead of them, all the way out to BC, but they couldn't afford to skip those, not if they hoped to get back into the pros by July.

Of course, spending their free time with Carson's family was not at all what Tracy had in mind. Not that she planned anything much. She thought about going home to Coaldale and checking in on her dad, but something about that didn't appeal very much to her. Not that she didn't want to see him; she missed him terribly, but Coaldale itself created the hesitance in her.

Fieldstone Ranch, with Vince and Rayna, was another option, but not one she really wanted to pursue. It felt healthy to distance herself from them, just like it did with Coaldale.

Where do I belong? she thought, rolling onto her side and drawing her blankets closer around her. She shivered and thought about Carson sleeping in the stock trailer. He must have been freezing. These spring nights were cold, and she had her heater running. He had nothing, not even insulated walls; although he claimed his sleeping bag was winter rated.

Where do I belong? she thought again. Here, on the road. That was an easy answer. But she couldn't stay on the road forever. Reality was: her pro rodeo days were limited to however long her youth held out, or her body. Then there was the senior circuit, but she couldn't hope to make a living that way. Ranching? She didn't have enough money for land, nor did it appeal to her. And then there was November through March, five long months of nothing. She had to find a place to park her trailer, board her horse, and earn some cash, and the only thing she knew for sure was that it wouldn't be Coaldale this year. Maybe never again.

Now, there was the whole problem of meeting Carson's parents. She never should have agreed to that. But when she saw the look of panic mixed with disappointment on Carson's face, she couldn't let him down. He had a way of appealing to her soft side. But she wasn't good with parents. Shawn's parents always hated her, even before she tore out his heart and trampled it... multiple times. If Carson's parents hated her, it could very well mean the end of their relationship, and therefore their working relationship, and her best chance at making it to the championships.

Of course, if she brought up her concerns, he'd only reassure her that his parents' opinions didn't matter and tell her he cared about her. All men say that, but the fact remains: if the family doesn't like the girlfriend, it's only a matter of time before she's packing her bags. And even though it had only been a few weeks, she wasn't ready for that. And neither was their relationship. It was too fresh and new to withstand parental scrutiny.

I'm doing the right thing. For us, and for our careers, she thought. But she was trying to convince herself more than anyone else. The look of disappointment on Carson's face when she said she didn't want them to know she was his girlfriend nearly tore her apart. And if it weren't for the rodeo circuit, she probably would have gone along with it. But there was too much riding on the relationship lasting at least a few more months, to add family into the dynamic. Once all this was over, and they had their pro status, and were finished with the rodeo finals in November…

Once they got through November, then they could tell.

CHAPTER FIFTEEN

Tracy followed Carson's truck off the paved highway and onto a gravel road. Her hands shook a bit, so she clutched the steering wheel tighter. She had nothing to be afraid of. Carson wanted the same things she did; and that meant he wouldn't abandon her, no matter how the week went. But she just couldn't shake the fact that parents didn't usually like her.

Carson's family farm was the first one on the left. The house was set close to the road, and there wasn't much of a yard, mostly just some grass growing between the house and road. Everything beside and behind the house made up a gravel parking pad. Just a typical farm: *waste not* was the main theme here. The land was strictly for working, not for ornamental, pretty yards. Then again, it wasn't very different for ranchers. It was an attitude Tracy was familiar with—though not one she completely subscribed to. She enjoyed nature for what it was; and believed some of it should be left wild and free.

She parked beside Carson's truck and trailer, backing it in with practiced ease.

Turning off the rumbling diesel truck, she closed her eyes and drew in a deep breath. She kept drawing it in until her lungs reached max capacity, and then let it out as slowly as she could. That was her ritual before a run, something she learned many years ago to squelch her nerves. But it wasn't working now.

Tap, tap, tap.

She opened her eyes and looked out her window. Carson stood there, grinning like he was making fun of her for being scared. Fine, she'd show him! Unbuckling her seatbelt, she threw the door open, forcing Carson to jump out of the way.

"Ready?"

"Yep," she answered defiantly before putting her hat on and following him toward the ranch-style bungalow.

He didn't bother knocking, but opened the door and walked in. She followed behind, feeling hesitant, but fully determined not to show it.

"Hello?" he called out. "We're here."

An older woman, who Tracy assumed was Carson's mother, poked her head into the boot room. She smiled as she walked the rest of the way through the doorway, wiping her hands on a dishtowel. "Welcome! So glad you two made it. And making yourself right at home already, I see," she said, with a grin plastered on her face. Her eyes fell on Tracy and she looked worried. The merciless look of what Tracy guessed was disapproval filled her eyes, and her voice sounded high-pitched and tight.

This was a bad idea, thought Tracy, her resolve melting away rapidly.

"I'm Tracy." She extended her hand, and his mother took it, her smile much warmer this time.

"Joyce. I'm afraid my husband, Rod, is still out on the fields, but he should be back soon, and then we can have some lunch."

Carson dropped his bag on the floor, now that the introductions were over. He covered the distance between his mom and him in three large strides and pulled her up into a hug.

"Mom, please tell me you have some home-cooked food waiting. I'm starving."

Joyce stepped back and swatted her son, then walked out of the boot room and into the kitchen. "As soon as your father gets back. Lunch is nothing special, but I've got some ribs marinating for supper, and for once, your sister will be home to join us. When I told her you'd be here, she cancelled her plans with Jeremy right away."

She spoke while busying herself, allowing Carson and Tracy to enter the kitchen and find a place to sit around the table. At the mention of his sister, Tracy shot him a look. He never mentioned anything about a sister. She was even worse at getting along with sisters than she was with parents. If this week did anything, it would surely doom Carson and her.

"You never told me you had a sister."

"Oh, yes, Carson has four sisters."

"*Four?*" her eyes widened and she looked at him. No wonder he could handle all her ups and downs and stubbornness; he'd grown up in a house full of women. Nothing she threw at him would have been anything new. Problem was: a house full of women could easily see right through her. They wouldn't miss the surreptitious looks they'd share when they thought no one was looking, and feel duty bound to express their concerns over his relationship. A mother or father would quietly harbor their disapproval, while a sister could openly talk.

He shrugged. "Yeah, but only one is around right now. Two are in college and the other is living in Manitoba."

"Please don't tell me you're the youngest too."

"Nope, I'm the oldest. The youngest is the one who'll be over later. She's in grade twelve and still lives at home. You'll like her."

"I'm sure I will."

Joyce looked up, frowning while observing her son and his guest. Tracy smiled, standing up. "Anything I can help you with?"

"Oh, no. Sit down, please. You're my guest. What would you like to drink?"

"Uh, water would be good."

"Carson, get your friend a glass of water," she commanded, walking away.

"She's a busy woman, isn't she?" Tracy stared after her as she disappeared down the hall.

"Never stops." Carson walked over to the water cooler beside the fridge and poured her a glass, then went into the fridge and pulled out a beer, cracking it open.

Handing her the water, he chuckled. "I didn't think you were much of a water drinker."

She looked at the beer and shrugged. *That looks really good.* "Just trying to put my best foot forward."

He walked over, looking around before planting a quick kiss on her lips and hastily putting a little distance between them again. "They're going to love you, don't worry."

The back door slammed shut and a groan came from the back room.

"Hey, Dad!" called Carson.

A minute later, a man just as tall and thin as Carson walked in. If it weren't for the age gap, they'd have been identical. Height, build, face, hair—although Rod's was greyer than brown at this point—even the way they carried themselves was exactly the same.

"Glad to see you made it home all right," Rod said, emphasizing the word *home*. "This your friend?" he asked in a clipped sentence, tipping his head toward Tracy.

If she were feeling inferior to Joyce, Rod made her feel like a bug underfoot. *Your friend.* He couldn't even speak directly to her? She could already feel his condemnation rolling off him in waves.

"Yeah, this is Tracy. She's an incredible roper, Dad, you should see her."

He grunted, walking over to the sink to wash his hands.

Joyce walked back in. "Oh good, you're here. Go sit down. I have sandwiches and iced tea ready to serve."

Tracy removed her hat, hung it up in the boot room, and then sat down at the table across from Carson. Her eyes met his, which seemed to twinkle. He looked happy, *really* happy.

I'm in way over my head, Tracy thought glumly.

* * *

After lunch, Joyce chased them out of the house, politely refusing Tracy's offer to help with dishes. Outside, they walked over to the corrals where Jack and Danny-boy quietly grazed from a bale feeder. Tracy held her hat in her hand, and clamped it down on her head as they stood there.

"Now what?"

Carson shrugged. "Wanna go for a ride?"

"'Cause we don't live on horses enough as it is?"

"It's that, or we help my mom around the house."

As much as she wanted to be a good guest and help out, the idea of spending the afternoon with Joyce was… terrifying. "Riding sounds great."

Tracy and Carson always competed with each other, even racing to see who could tack up faster. So far, Tracy usually won. But every once in a while, Carson managed to beat her, usually when Jack refused to stand still, or be caught.

Today was a good day, though, and she managed to mount up just as he finished tightening the latigo.

"Where to, cowboy?"

Carson's tacit reply was to ride off, but not before tipping his head for her to follow. Fine, if he wanted to be that way, she was okay with it. She felt glad to be riding outside of an arena, for once. Riding within the confines of the rodeo grounds got very tiring after doing it day in and day out. She could tell by Jack's attitude that he needed to get out on the open plains again. He'd been living in stalls, the trailer, and an arena for the past month. Sure, when the rodeo grounds were quiet, she and Carson let the horses run free in the arena where they could kick up their hooves and roll, but it wasn't the same. If she were beginning to feel cooped up, she could only imagine how her gelding felt.

Tracy followed Carson as he rode toward the highway. Normally, they would chat during practice, or flatwork, but

Carson seemed to understand she liked to enjoy the scenery during trail rides. It was about shutting down and closing out the world, or maybe, letting the real world in.

She leaned back in her saddle as they rode down the steep grade of the last huge coulee just before entering town. Instead of continuing up the other side, Carson turned left and proceeded further down the valley.

Tracy squeezed the sides of her feet into Jack's belly and he moved up into a slow jog, pulling up beside Carson.

Even beside each other, they remained quiet. Tracy glanced over at him. He looked peaceful... happy even. The man she'd gotten to know on the circuit was driven and competitive. This man, however, was relaxed and calm.

"You don't actually want to leave here, do you?"

He looked at her, and a frown marred his face. "Why would you say that?"

"Because you're so obviously at peace here."

Laughter exploded from him. "Peace? I've been here for what? A grand total of two hours? I'm on vacation mode. Believe me, once I've been here for twenty-four hours, I'll be anything but relaxed."

She smiled. "So this place is your Coaldale."

"Except I'm not running away."

A thick, stale silence fell over them. Yeah, she was running away, but not from anyone or anything. She was just running away from herself, and that wasn't exactly something she could ever accomplish.

"That's not fair."

"Sorry, but it is true. You'd rather face my family, and be absolutely terrified, than go home and visit your own dad."

"I'm not running from Coaldale. I'm just not ready to go back yet."

She glanced over to see him grinning. It's not like she said anything funny, but there he sat, looking smug and proud of himself, and she hated it. Almost enough to send her packing back to Coaldale *just* to prove him wrong. But she tried proving him wrong earlier today, when facing his family, and only succeeded in making a horrible first impression.

"I'm done talking. Let's just go back to the silence thing."

"Whatever you say, cowgirl."

CHAPTER SIXTEEN

"Carson!"

He lifted his hat when his sister ran out of the house. After dismounting, he left the reins over Danny's neck and held out his arms. Carly didn't miss a beat as she flew into them. Twirling her around, he laughed. "You'd think I was gone for years, and not just a month."

"A month too long! You left me here all alone with Mom and Dad."

He laughed. Carly loved it at home, although she often pretended she didn't. She was the best bet their dad had of passing the farm on to a family member. His other sisters moved out of town as soon as they could, leaving only Carly and him behind. And with the way things were going with Tracy now, Carson didn't really think he'd be coming back.

"Oh, Carly," he said, putting her down, while turning to check on Tracy. She was still sitting on her horse, looking a little lost. "I want you to meet Tracy."

"*You* brought a girl home?"

He couldn't contain his grin. Leave it to Carly to mention he hadn't brought a girl home in… forever. He looked back at Tracy, and she gave him a raised eyebrow and a crooked smile. Yeah, she didn't miss a thing.

"Just my rodeo partner," he replied, giving her a wink. He never could lie to Carly, not that he ever had to. Just knowing he had a girl, a real, live girl at home, would send her over the moon. And if he tried to hide the relationship from her, she'd, no doubt, call him out on it at the most inopportune time. Better to let her in on the secret now.

Her eyes widened and he glimpsed the beginnings of an excited squeal. "We just rope together," he explained, to further suggest they should not talk about anything else involving Tracy and him.

"Mmmhmmm, that must be… nice." She glanced over his shoulder at Tracy, who still waited quietly for his intimate moment with his sister to end.

"Hi, Tracy. Nice to meet you." She waved, and then turned, her perfectly straightened hair fanning the air as she flounced off toward the house again.

A hand touched his shoulder and he turned around. Tracy looked gorgeous, especially when she got mad. The way her brow furrowed and her eyes flashed, not to mention, the upturning of her lips told him he was in for a few choice words.

"Should we find someplace private to have a discussion?"

She shrugged, not saying a word as she walked away. He had two choices: follow her, or put Danny away as quickly as possible before retreating to the safe confines of his parents' home. She wouldn't dare call him out for spilling their silly, little secret. But either way, they'd have to discuss the subject at some point. Better sooner than later. He followed her, untacking Danny and putting him in the corral. Tracy was already done, and waited with her hands on her hips.

"I'm going to walk into my trailer. Feel free to follow."

His saddle still in hand, Carson deposited it in his trailer before following her into the RV.

"Okay, let's have it. You're mad."

Tracy was in her room. The door to her bathroom was closed, now that he replaced it with a new, solid door, instead of the hollow-cored one that he crashed through a few weeks ago.

"I'm not mad," her voice drifted through the closed door right before it opened. She changed clothes, and her hair hung loose again. He liked her hair down, but she rarely wore it that way. "I just… you know, I'm not ready for your family to know."

"Carly is my sister."

"She's a teenager, who will talk."

"She'll stay quiet, I promise. You saw how excited she was over the prospect of me dating someone… Even if I lied, she'd see right through it."

Tracy's lips pressed together in a straight line and she nodded. "Your parents don't like me much, do they?"

How many people ever saw this vulnerable, unsure side of Tracy? He was pretty sure she kept it safely locked away, deep inside. Yet for some reason, she chose to reveal it to him. "I'm pretty sure they haven't drawn any conclusions about you yet. I'd give it at least until after dinner. Can we please not talk about my family for just five seconds?"

She walked over and snaked her arms around his neck, pressing closer to him, and instantly leaving him powerless to think, or continue the conversation. "Hey, cowboy?"

"Yeah?" he whispered, his lips hovering just above hers.

"Kiss me."

* * *

Tracy helped Carly clear the table after dinner, at her insistence; and finally, after being persuaded by Carson and his dad, Joyce eventually relaxed for the evening. She poured a glass of wine and left the clean-up to the younger women.

Carly filled the dishwasher while Tracy brought her plates.

"So, you and my brother?"

Tracy didn't miss a beat. "Yeah, but we're trying to keep it quiet, for now. It's still pretty new." She was expecting that conversation to come up sooner or later. At least, Carly waited until they had a moment alone.

Carly grinned, her eyes dancing with excitement. "He seems pretty happy."

"I think it's because he's living out his dreams."

"And maybe it has a little something to do with you."

She closed the dishwasher, pressing some buttons before it rumbled to life, drowning out their conversation.

"Here's the thing; Carson hasn't had many girlfriends, and brought even fewer home. Even if this whole thing is new, it definitely must mean something to *him*."

Tracy swallowed, nodding. She knew she'd have to stick it out at least until November, not that she was looking for an escape. Everything was going well, but it wasn't supposed to be serious. Not yet. Not so soon.

"I'm not going to hurt him."

Carly shrugged and poured herself a glass of water. "Girls like you tend to hurt guys like my brother. If you're the real deal, then I'm happy for you guys, and we're cool. But if you're not..." she trailed off, but didn't need to say the words. Tracy understood loud and clear. If she hurt Carson, they'd destroy her in this town.

Oh well, just one more to wipe off my list of potential places to call home, she thought.

"I care about your brother a lot."

"Good."

She walked into the living room to join her family. Standing in the doorway of the kitchen, Tracy surveyed them. Joyce sat reading while sipping on a glass of red wine. Carson and his dad were in front of the TV, watching *Sports Center* and occasionally voicing a protest or two. Carly plopped down on the floor at Carson's feet and leaned against him, pulling out her phone and tapping away at the screen with her thumbs.

The room seemed comfortable, peaceful even. Everyone was doing their own thing, yet they were meshed. They were one unit, as in tune with each other as the hand is with the foot or the head. Tracy never really understood the term *family unit* until then.

"Hey, Tracy, grab a seat," said Carson, looking over.

"I think I'm going to call it a night. I'm pretty beat."

Carson frowned. She was a night owl and he knew it. She couldn't hide her discomfort from him, but she also needed to be alone, and sought more space just to breathe.

"Okay. I'll see you in the morning," he replied. No one else even so much as looked over. Rather than grabbing their attention to say good night, she quietly left the house.

Instead of going straight into her trailer, she walked over to the small corral that contained hers and Carson's horses. There wasn't any pasture reserved for the horses here, or at least, none that she noticed. But it also appeared that Carson was the only one who owned a horse in the household. That seemed strange. Usually, in small farming and ranching towns, everyone and their dog owned horses, even people who never rode them.

She leaned on the fence, listening to the frogs croaking and the crunching of hay in the horses' mouths.

Out there, calm soon befell her. She didn't even realize how stiff and uncomfortable she felt until it all melted away out there in the open air. So, rather than going to bed like she said she was, she climbed into the corral and walked over to Jack. Placing her hands on his withers and tangling her fingers in his mane, she jumped up onto the horse's bare back. Settling down, she stroked his neck, then draped herself across it, taking in his sweet, horsey smell.

She laid there, her mind replaying the events of the last few weeks. Was Carly right? Was Carson in deep already? And how did she feel about him? They worked well together, and the attraction was alive and strong, stronger now than it ever was. She really couldn't imagine leaving him; but that's not to say it wouldn't change in another month or two. She wasn't ready to commit to forever, not yet, but his sister seemed to think that Carson was almost there.

She heard a light rapping sound, and looked up to see Carson standing outside her trailer door, knocking.

"Over here," she called out, sitting up so she wouldn't blend in totally with the horse.

He looked around and his eyes settled on her. It was dark, but she could tell he wasn't happy. His walk lacked energy and his shoulders slumped a bit.

He slipped through the rails and walked over, resting his hand on her leg.

"Are you so uncomfortable with my family that you would rather be alone out here?"

She closed her eyes, searching for the right words to reply. She had to be careful; she didn't want to start a fight, not now. "I just needed some alone time is all."

"I get that, but you make new friends wherever we go, Tracy. What is it about my family that has you so... on edge?"

She sighed. "Nothing. They seem really nice. I just feel under a lot of pressure to impress them, you know?" He nodded. "Carly is really sweet, though. She gave me *the talk*."

"The talk?"

"Yeah, you know; if you hurt my brother, I'll kill you."

Laughter erupted from deep within him and he planted his hands on her hips, pulling her off Jack and into his arms.

"And?"

"And what?"

"Am I at risk of being hurt?"

"Never, cowboy." And *that* she meant.

If anything, I'll be the one walking away from all this with a broken heart, she thought, but kept it to herself.

CHAPTER SEVENTEEN

Two Months Later

Rodeo after rodeo, drive after drive, win or lose, every event seemed to blend into the next one. They traveled across Western Canada and back again, steadily racking up the points.

Sitting outside her trailer at the Airdrie, Alberta rodeo grounds, Tracy sipped her beer and browsed her phone, looking at their standings.

"If we come in first, we can apply to the pro association."

"So soon?" asked Carson, his shock apparent on his face.

"Yeah, we've been doing really well. I don't think I've ever had a run of luck this good before."

"Which means, it has to run out sooner or later," he grumbled.

"Not this weekend, it won't. We just gotta get through this one last run before we take a bit of a break."

A *break*; it sounded heavenly. It wouldn't be a long one, with only a few short months to work their way up to the rodeo finals in November. Just long enough for them and their horses to recuperate before the craziness of the big rodeos began.

The end goal, the goal that she kept her eyes on, was the rodeo finals, though. She'd gone a few times, but never done well. This year was supposed to be *the year*, and it *would* be the year she would take team roping champion. She and Carson worked well together. They were completely in sync. He didn't take her crap, and she didn't need to give him any. She couldn't have picked a better partnership. But things were becoming tense. With every buckle they won, and their steadily growing points and bank accounts, the pressure grew greater and weighed heavier on them. Their goals were now within their grasp.

"What's wrong?" she asked. Carson stayed quiet all night, which wasn't really unlike him. But it was a sulking quiet. His answers were short and clipped, and he mumbled a lot, while glowering.

"Nothing."

There it was; the single, clipped response. And even that seemed to take too much effort from him.

She sighed. "Something is wrong. Now, will you talk to me? Or should I just leave you here to mope?"

"We don't talk about anything else." The words jumbled out of him in a rush.

"What?"

"We only talk about the rodeo. We only talk about making it to the finals. Nothing else. What happens after November? What happens if we don't make it?"

"We will make it. We have lots of time."

"That's not what I mean! What happens to us? The only thing gluing us together is this." He spread his hands out to emphasize his words.

Tracy's heart sunk. This was what she feared, this was why she insisted on keeping everything about the rodeo; she didn't want to complicate their partnership with their relationship. Not until after the finals anyway. Then they'd have all winter to figure out where they were going as a couple. "What's so wrong with that? We just take things one step at a time."

"One step at a time doesn't give me a lot of hope for our future. What's the big picture here?"

She frowned, taking a deep breath and attempting to expand her tightening chest.

"I can't think about us right now, Carson. Rodeo is my life. Rodeo is my future. Once my future is secure, we can talk about us. For now, can't you just be happy knowing that I care about you?"

He shook his head. "And what happens if we don't make it? Do you do what's best for your life and leave me?"

"I can't believe we're having this conversation right now! We're one win away from reaching our goals, and you're stirring up drama where there doesn't need to be any."

"I'm not trying to stir up drama, Tracy. I just want to understand what we are. What I mean to you."

He looked so sad and wistful that her anger fizzled out and left her feeling empty. She sighed, took a sip of her beer, and stood up. "I want us to work just as much as you do, Carson. I promise. But right now, we need to keep our eyes on our goals, okay? Let's just get through this weekend and then maybe, we can take some time off together to figure the other things out."

"I want you to come to Foremost again with me."

She shook her head. "I can't promise that right now."

He looked disappointed, but nodded. "Are you going home?"

She shrugged. "I think so. I haven't seen my dad in a while, and a little space might be good for the two of us. We haven't been apart in three months."

Walking toward the stall blocks, she left Carson sitting alone under the awning of her trailer.

* * *

Carson watched Tracy walk away. He was an idiot. Could he have had worse timing? She was right, they needed to just get through this weekend and then they'd be home free. The pressure would be off, and there would be plenty of time for them to figure things out.

But he couldn't help feeling they were stuck in a rut. Two months had passed since they visited his home in Foremost, and he still couldn't forget how uncomfortable she was with his family. The only one she got along with was Carly. She kept his parents at arm's length, spending as little time with them as possible. Maybe he was wrong to push her into meeting his family so early in their relationship, but it scared him when she showed no interest in making any effort. If they were to have any future together, she had to get along with his family. He couldn't imagine leaving her, but he couldn't walk away from his family either, not even for a woman as incredible as Tracy.

Draining his beer, he walked out toward the rodeo stands, his mind still fastened on Tracy.

They spent all their time together, yet they didn't. Their trailers were parked right beside each other, but they ate as many meals separately as together. Most of the time, they drove alone, and when they were together, they just talked rodeo. Bills, income, strategy, what they had to improve on…. their lives revolved around it.

I should have known better than to mix business with pleasure, he thought, kicking at a patch of gravel.

But it was too late to change things now. He couldn't go back to being just partners, or even being just friends with Tracy. Every time he thought about her, he couldn't envision his future without her. He couldn't imagine doing a circuit without her. And he'd have done anything to keep what they had, even if it meant staying in that rut forever.

Well, maybe not forever, because eventually, you either got out, or a whole lot of shit got spun up from underneath. But he intended to stay here as long as she needed to, and then fight to keep her.

"Hey, Carson!"

He looked over to see Fred, one of the cowboys he befriended on the road. He waved Carson over from the practice ring fence.

He walked over, joining his friend. Inside a horse breathed heavily, and his chest and rump shone with sweat. It was a beautiful steed though, a flashy tobiano paint with the muscles of a cow horse.

"What's his story?"

"I picked him up from an auction last week. He's going to be my next cutting horse. Want to take a spin on him?"

Carson shrugged. "Looks like he might still have some fight."

Fred shook his head. "Not really. Curly, here, ran him through all his paces. He seems steady enough."

Carson pursed his lips together, pulling his hat down a little lower over his face to block out the sun. He studied the horse as Curly dismounted and led him over to the fence.

"Yeah, sure, I'll try him out."

Hefting himself up and over the metal fencing, Carson jumped down on the other side. He accepted the reins from Curly and patted the horse on his shoulder, watching him. He looked calm enough, even tired.

"Watch him on the transition into canter. He likes to fight that a little."

"Thanks, man."

Carson gripped the cantle with one hand and the mane in the other, hopping up and down, counting in his head, then pulling his body up and swinging his leg over, settling into the saddle. The gelding danced a little, but calmed down when Carson didn't give in. Adjusting his reins, Carson waited a moment, then requested a walk with a click of his tongue and a slight squeeze from his boots.

The horse moved off, hesitating for the first couple of steps, but steadying to a nice, even gait after another cluck from his rider. Keeping him on a smaller circle, rather than giving him the whole practice ring, Carson urged him into a jog. The horse's head flew up and he moved off with more energy and pep than Carson would've liked, but he just sat deeper, rolling his wrists down to put just a little pressure on the bit. The horse dropped his head and his jog smoothed out.

"Nice mover," he said as he passed by the fence where Fred and Curly stood.

Readjusting his seat and checking his reins, Carson shifted his weight to encourage the right lead, and asked the horse to once again, move up.

Sure enough, the gelding gave a little kickback of disapproval, causing a little bump in the ride, but with no other protest, he slipped into a nice, smooth canter.

Just one nice circuit and we'll call it a day, Carson thought, moving with the rocking motion of the horse.

The horse moved forward, and Carson felt his body jerk into the air before landing heavily in the saddle. Second instinct had his hand gripping the saddle horn and mane as the horse's body contracted beneath him like a loaded spring.

"Where did that come from!" he yelled, giving the horse a kick to move him forward and out of the buck.

The gelding shook his head and bounced up on his front feet, ignoring Carson's commands.

"Move off," he commanded through clenched teeth, giving the horse another kick as it tucked his head down for another buck.

He needed to get off before he got hurt, but he couldn't do that until he calmed down the horse.

This time the horse moved forward, but rather than dropping into a controlled gait, he stretched out his neck and ran. Carson took a deep breath, willing his pounding heart to slow down.

"Whoa," he said in a calm voice, while inside, he felt anything but calm. Bucking he could handle, taking off at an uncontrolled gallop was a lot harder to cling to.

The horse zigged left, and Carson's body went right, but he still managed to stay in the seat. Finding his center again, he reached down the rein and pulled the horse's head to his knee. The horse's hind end spun around, still resisting the stop that his rider tried to impose on him.

"Whoa," he uttered again. "Whoa, boy."

Everything shifted beneath him, and he could feel the horse's legs slipping out. Kicking his feet out of the stirrups, Carson released the reins simultaneously and jumped off to the right, landing hard in the sand. The breath whooshed out of his chest just as a crushing weight landed on his left leg. Almost as soon as it was there, it was gone again, and he looked up to see the horse running off across the arena. Curly and Fred had already jumped over the fence to catch the free horse.

"Carson! Are you okay?"

He sat up, brushing the sand off his shoulder and noticed Tracy running across the arena to him.

"Fine. You saw that?"

"The end of it." She offered her hand.

He accepted it and winced as he stood up. Putting his left foot down, pain shot up his ankle, through his leg, and ended somewhere in his hip. He slumped back down with a hiss of air escaping his lips.

"You're not fine," she said, kneeling down beside him and removing his boot.

"Probably just twisted it. I'll be fine."

"That horse fell on you. You're getting this checked out."

He let Tracy help him onto his feet again, this time being more careful not to put any weight on his left foot. Instead, he hunched over and leaned on her for support, limping along to the fence line where she deposited him near the gate.

"I'll go get the truck; just wait here."

Carson sat, watching her jog away toward their trucks. He closed his eyes and mentally kicked himself. *How could I be so dumb? We had everything in our grasp, everything! And now we'll have to scratch tomorrow.*

"You okay, Carson?"

He looked up at Fred and the paint horse he had in tow.

"I'll be fine. Don't worry about me."

"That was quite the ride. If the horse hadn't lost his footing, you would have had him."

"Sometimes, that's just the way it turns out," he muttered.

Fred pursed his lips and nodded before leading the horse away. Carson grimaced as the throbbing in his leg escalated. He picked up his boot that lay in the sand beside him and threw it to the side. Anger coursed through him; not toward the horse, but mostly at himself for mounting a strange horse right before a competition.

Tracy's truck rolled up and she jumped down, walking around to help him into the passenger seat. Once settled in the truck, she drove off without a word. The Airdrie regional hospital wasn't far, and the emergency room would be open and have X-ray capabilities. That's all they needed right now. Answers.

Time seemed to move in slow motion as Tracy helped him from place-to-place, finally getting him seated in the clinic waiting room while she checked him in.

"They'll see us in a couple of minutes," she muttered.

He could see the concern in her eyes, but her tone of voice told him that the reality of the situation had already begun to sink in.

He answered the doctor's questions with barely a thought, moving robotically as the X-rays were taken, and sitting on the table in the exam room to await the news he already knew. He wouldn't be walking anytime soon.

"It looks like a hairline fracture of your tibia," said the doctor, walking in. "We'll cast it and I'll give you the radiographs to take to your own doctor for a follow-up in a couple of weeks. But I'm sorry to say you won't be riding anytime soon."

Carson nodded, already resigned to that fact.

"Thank you, Doctor," answered Tracy on his behalf.

Sitting in the truck, parked beside his trailer, they sat in utter silence.

"I'm sorry," he finally mumbled.

"I guess that's it," she replied. "We're done for the year."

"We still have plenty of time to make the finals," he said, trying to stay upbeat when all he wanted to do was punch something.

"Not enough time, not after you heal."

"I know," he whispered.

"How could you be so stupid?" she said, suddenly turning on him, her eyes flashing, rimmed red from threatening tears. "How could you get up on a strange horse?"

He hated seeing her like that, broken and upset. He wanted more than anything to make her dreams come true. But he couldn't. He messed it all up by taking a risk he never should have, and now they both had to live with the consequences.

"Next year, Tracy. I promise."

He reached for her hand across the console, but she stiffened and pulled away from him.

"Tracy..." he trailed off. He didn't know what to say to make everything better. He couldn't. He knew that. Tracy wanted to make the finals more than anything, it consumed her. There was no way around it; she wasn't going to make it this year because of him. It was all his fault.

He opened the door of the truck and wrestled his crutches out, lowering himself to the ground. "I'm sorry, Tracy. I really am," he said, then closed the door.

She didn't even meet his eyes. She turned off the truck and climbed out, walking toward her own trailer and slamming the door shut. He still stood there, watching, leaning his weight on the crutches. Digging his cellphone out, he dialed a number he knew by heart.

"Hi, Dad. I need you to come pick me up. I'm hurt."

CHAPTER EIGHTEEN

Tracy emerged from her trailer hours later after taking a nap, and looked around. The rodeo grounds were still abuzz with people milling through the stands, talking, and some doing evening chores.

She walked over to the stalls, stopping outside Jack's. Danny's was located right beside his, but it was empty. Peering inside, she saw it hadn't been cleaned and the water pail still hung, while loose hay remained in the corner, and an entire unopened bale sat outside.

He must have gotten someone to exercise Danny, she thought.

Going about her evening chores, she filled Jack's water pail and gave him some more hay for the night. Chores were therapeutic and allowed her to calm down, while accessing the situation from a more logical perspective. Carson was right, there was always next year for the finals. This year, she had to concentrate on getting him into the professional association so that he could continue doing it, instead of returning to his dad's farm. They could get one or two rodeos in this season after he healed up, and he'd need her around to do that.

She mucked out Jack's stall into a wheelbarrow and hefted it up onto its wheel, pausing outside Danny's stall. He still wasn't back. She walked in and scooped out the manure.

Maybe Carson would see that as the apology she meant for it to be. She'd been horrible to him, pushing off their relationship, putting all the pressure on making the finals—an unattainable goal. They had a great season, and she owed a huge part of that to Carson. She never would have done as well as she did without him.

The water pail still looked pretty full, but she dumped it into the barrow of shavings and manure and filled it up fresh.

Dumping the barrow and putting it away, she pulled out her phone and dialed her dad's number—one of the few numbers she actually knew from memory.

"Hey, girly." His voice sounded comforting when he answered the phone.

"Hey, Dad. I," she paused, not really sure if she should just spit it out, or make small talk first.

"You aren't going to make it to the finals."

"Not this year. I got close, though. Real close. I have an amazing header, really talented and consistent. Thanks to him I got this far." She smiled, thinking about Carson. She would make it up to him; take him to dinner, apologize, and maybe even watch the Calgary stampede before heading back on the road.

"You found someone you can work with?"

"Yeah. Crazy, isn't it?"

"I'll say. Don't let him go! I don't think you'll ever find another."

"Dad!"

She stopped. Staring at her trailer, or rather, past her trailer where Carson's truck and trailer were usually parked. It was gone.

"I have to call you back," she said, hanging up the phone without waiting for his response.

Walking around her trailer, as if maybe she just walked up at a bad angle, she stopped and stared at the empty spot. He left, without a word. He just packed up and drove off, leaving everything the way it was.

Her stomach roiled, and her breath hitched.

There has to be some explanation, she thought, scrolling through her list of contacts until she got to his name. She pressed send and the phone rang only twice before she got his voicemail.

"Fine, you want to ignore my call," she seethed, hanging up without leaving a message. She'd been mean, but not harsh enough to warrant him packing up and leaving her behind without another word. She'd just try again later, once his bruises had a little time to heal.

* * *

Carson stared at Tracy's name glowing on his phone's screen, then quickly pressed *end*. The ringing stopped, and the screen went dark again. He didn't expect her to take this long to call, but figured it was probably just to yell at him for skipping town without telling her.

He half expected his phone to buzz a *voicemail waiting* notification, but it remained silent and still. She was obviously upset, then. If she were calling to ask him to come back, she would have done so in a message.

"That her?" asked his dad from the driver's seat.

"Yep."

It took her long enough to even realize he was gone. He'd been on the road for two hours already. He'd be home in another two, and then he could start putting Tracy behind him and figuring out what to do next.

Maybe it was time to leave his dreams of the rodeo behind. He had an amazing three months, but the ups and downs, the stress, and the toll it took on what could have been a great thing between Tracy and him—he was beginning to think wasn't worth all that. Maybe he should just settle down and help his dad run the farm. It's not like the thought hadn't crossed his mind before, but he never wanted to get serious about it. Especially when the prospect of him going on the road still loomed ahead. He couldn't have lived with the *what ifs*. He couldn't imagine his future without Tracy, but maybe he could without the rodeo.

The drive went by in complete silence. His dad pulled the truck and trailer into their yard and backed the rig in, unloading Danny without a word as Carson stood and watched, completely helpless on his crutches. He looked up at the sound of footsteps crunching on gravel.

"I didn't know you were coming home. What did you do?"

He smiled at Carly and swung his body into motion with the use of his crutches. "Surprise, little sister."

She fell into step beside him, walking toward the house. She glanced around. "Where's Tracy?"

He grunted. Leave it to his sister to bring up the one topic he preferred not to talk about.

"Not here, I take it?"

"Don't worry about Tracy. You have your big brother again for a few weeks now, and I didn't come back to talk about her."

Carly went quiet, but he could see her stiffening. She was reading between the lines, lines that he didn't need anyone reading between. Tracy was so right; he shouldn't have let anyone know about them. It would have been a whole lot simpler. Now he had to deal with his sister's immediate dislike for her, and that wasn't fair. None of this was Tracy's fault. He let her down, and held her back. At least, his parents wouldn't know any better; and he could chalk things up to their business arrangement no longer working out due to his injury.

"I, uh, have to make a call. I'll catch up with you later, okay?"

Carly stopped and turned to look at him, a frown marring her youthful face. She wore more makeup than he would have liked to see, and it made her look older than she was. She needed to hold onto her youth as long as she could. It wasn't complicated. There were no life-altering decisions, and relationships weren't serious.

"Catch up with me later?"

"I'll come into the house after I finish my call."

"Why can't you just come and say hi? Make the phone call later? If you're going to call Tracy—"

"I'm not," he cut her off. "Fine, I'll come say hello first. But, Carly…"

"Yeah?"

"Don't be all upset over Tracy. She didn't hurt me… I screwed up, okay?"

"You can tell me about it later."

She opened the door to the boot room and let him go in first.

"Mom! Carson and Dad are back," she yelled out, kicking off her shoes with her toe and walking into the kitchen.

He lowered himself to the bench and leaned his crutches against the wall. He removed his boot just as his mom came through the door and enveloped him in a hug right where he sat.

"I'm so glad you're okay. When you said you were hurt, you had me thinking the worst," she rambled on in a hurry.

"You should let me go before you add smothering to my list of injuries."

She stepped back and studied him. "It's just the leg?"

"I'm fine, Mom. Just a fracture. I'll be back on my feet before you know it."

"Good." She handed him his crutches and went back through the doorway into the kitchen. He missed that, the playfulness, and the love. There wasn't any stress here, unlike with the rodeo, or Tracy.

Then why can't I think about anything but her? he thought. Plastering on a smile, he walked over to the table, spun a chair around and sat on it, leaning back with the leg in a cast stretched out. "It's good to be home."

* * *

"Can we talk?" asked Carly, walking out across the lawn to join Carson who was sitting underneath a tree. He flipped his phone open, then closed it. Three more calls from Tracy, but still not a single message.

He looked up at his sister, her long hair pulled up into one of those bun things that sat on top of her head. It was cute, and made her look more her age. Patting the ground beside him, he nodded. "What's up?"

"You seem upset. You didn't just come here because you're hurt, or did you?"

He shrugged. "I couldn't exactly stay on the rodeo circuit like this. It wouldn't be fair to ask Tracy to babysit me."

She snorted. "Sure, and this has nothing to do with you feeling guilty over riding that horse? Did she get mad at you?"

He told his family about the horse over supper, and left things at that. "A little, but not much. That's part of the problem. She should be mad. No, she should be furious. I derailed everything."

"And you just left? Judging by her phone calls, you didn't even say goodbye, did you? For being my big brother, you sure don't have a lot of relationship smarts."

"Probably why I'm still single, squirt," he chuckled, wrapping his arm around her neck in a headlock.

"Hey! Let me go!" she yelled, struggling ineffectually. He wasn't holding her tight, though, and let her slip out.

"I was being serious. You really liked her; and now you're just going to walk away from her because you feel guilty?"

He flipped his phone open and closed, open and closed, over and over again. "I didn't just let her down, okay? I ruined her chance at the finals. That was her dream. I don't expect you to understand."

"I'm not that young. I've had a relationship or two, and been through a few fights, made more than my share of mistakes, and even have some experience with regret. I'm old enough to understand."

He sighed, tossing his phone to her. She flipped it open and looked at the screen he kept staring at. The call logs. Four missed calls, all from Tracy.

"She obviously wants to talk to you."

He grunted. "Yeah, but about what?"

"If she's smart, to make sure your relationship is still intact. Only way to find out is if you actually answer the phone."

"Now isn't that a novel idea?"

She stood up, grunting a bit. "I'm not saying you should call her, I'm just saying answer her the next time the phone rings. It never hurts to hear what she has to say. She might just surprise you."

"You aren't supposed to take her side."

"I'm not. I'm taking yours. You just don't know it yet."

Carson grinned, waving his sister away. Maybe she was right, but he didn't know what he wanted to hear from Tracy yet, or what he'd say to her. If she really cared, she'd keep calling until he answered. And if not, she'd probably be better off without him anyway.

* * *

Tracy threw her phone onto the bed beside her and sighed, letting her hand fall and bounce on the lumpy mattress. The phone kept going to voicemail after only a couple of rings—he was still ignoring her calls. And to keep dialing his number bordered on pathetic.

She got up, picking up her phone, and slipping it into her pocket. On the off chance that he'd call her back, she wanted to keep it close by.

She walked into the kitchen and grabbed a bottle of water out of the fridge, sinking into her easy chair and flipping through the latest issue of *Horse Country* that she picked up at the grocery store magazine stand.

She flipped through, noticing the pictures, but failing to understand the words. She kept replaying the fight they had over and over in her head, wondering what she could say to fix things, and bring him back to her. Anything to hear his voice tell her he still cared about her.

"Life goes on," she chided herself, dumping the magazine on the small side table and digging her phone out of her pocket. Dialing a series of ten digits she had memorized, she listened to the phone ring.

"Trace, how's it going?"

"Hey, Shawn, got a minute?"

The line went silent.

"Shawn?"

"Yeah, I do. What's wrong?"

He could tell something was wrong just by the sound of her voice. How pathetic must she be? Sitting here moping, calling the one guy who always cared about her and had a smile on his face despite being continually rejected.

"Why do you still put up with me?"

"'Cause you're an incredible woman, Trace, and I want you to stay in my life."

"But why? I treat you like crap. I treat everyone like crap; and almost everyone takes off running. Just you and my dad, you're the only ones that stick around. Why?"

A sigh came again, and it sounded like Shawn was repositioning himself. Glancing at the clock on the microwave, she realized it was past midnight. "Oh, no! Did I wake you up?"

"Kind of."

"I'm so sorry. I shouldn't have bugged you."

"No, it's fine. I don't know why I stay. I know that's not the answer you're looking for, and I hate saying it, but I really don't. I guess I just can't turn off my feelings, you know?"

She thought about Carson and winced. Yeah, she knew. She knew all too well.

"I'm really sorry for the way I've been treating you all these years." She twirled a strand of hair between her fingers and bit her lip, holding back angry tears.

"Did something happen, Trace?"

She smiled and a tear rolled down her face. Swiping it away, she drew in a deep breath. "I chased Carson away." She laughed. "I guess it was only a matter of time."

"You weren't just roping partners, were you?"

"Nope."

"You really liked him?"

She choked back a sob, pressing the palm of her hand into her eyes, trying to stop the burning tears. She was really trying to hold it together.

"Hey, Trace, don't cry. Please. I'm sure whatever happened can be fixed. Just, please don't cry. You know I can't handle that."

"I'm sorry," she sputtered between tears. Now they flowed freely, and she hated herself for it.

"Call him."

"I tried."

"And?"

"He won't answer."

"Do you know where he went?"

"Home, probably." The one place, besides the middle of an abandoned rodeo arena, where she'd seen him relax, was at his parents' home. If he cared for her as much as she did for him, and if he was hurting as bad as she was, he'd run for familiar ground. And besides that, who else would have come and helped him pack up except his father?

"Go find him. Make him talk to you. Apologize for whatever you said or did. That guy has it bad for you."

She sniffled, wiping at her nose and eyes. "Just drop everything and find him?"

"Crazy, eh?"

"Yep."

"I'd do it if it meant I could have you."

She closed her eyes. His voice was pained, sad, like he just set down the torch he'd been carrying for years. And despite how much it hurt him to set it aside, he sounded a bit relieved. Like now that he knew she found someone, he could finally move on.

"Thank you, Shawn."

"For what?"

"For listening. For answering my call even though you were sleeping. For helping me, even though it probably hurts you to."

"I'd do anything for you, Trace. You know that."

She hated hearing those words. She hated that he said them; and hoped he could let them go. He needed to find someone who would appreciate his heart of gold, not someone like her who called on him whenever she needed help, but never gave him the one thing he needed or sought.

"You really should stop."

She hung up, putting the phone down slowly. Leaning forward, she pressed the heels of her hands into her eyes and sighed. Her tears dried up, right about the moment she realized that Shawn kept powering through life despite her continually destroying him. She had no right to feel sorry for herself.

But the tears that fell and dried left her skin feeling tight and her eyes tired. Getting up, she walked to the sink and splashed some water on her face, letting the cool liquid wash away her self-pity. Foremost was what? Four hours away? Five? She could pack up and be on the road in an hour, meaning she'd get there by six a.m. She looked at the microwave again where the time taunted her, the minutes ticking by. Pressing her lips together, she flicked on the coffee maker's —all prepped and on a timer for the morning.

CHAPTER NINETEEN

Tracy drove through the night, but somewhere along Highway 2, she decided to turn up the road to Coaldale instead of Foremost. Pulling into her dad's yard at five in the morning, her headlights washed over the house as she circled around and parked the truck out of the way.

Her entire body ached, and she guzzled about a pot of coffee over the last four hours, but even after that, she was fighting sleep. She kept telling herself that she hadn't chickened out, and needed to stop before she got into an accident, but the truth was that with every mile she drove, her apprehension grew inside her.

About the point when Coaldale appeared on the highway sign, her decision was made. She couldn't keep going. She wasn't going to be that pathetic woman who chased after a man only a few hours after he left her. If there was one thing she never did, it was beg. Already, she embarrassed herself enough by the amount of unanswered phone calls she made.

She unloaded Jack, putting him in an empty corral by the barn and walked back over to her trailer. She didn't bother to level it, or unhook it; she just climbed in for a few hours of sleep. Her dad would be up soon and want an explanation when he saw her. She needed sleep before facing that humiliation.

* * *

The sun hung high in the sky when Tracy opened her eyes again. She shook slightly, probably from the amount of caffeine she consumed last night mixed with a lack of sleep. Getting up, she walked out of the trailer, still fully dressed from the night before. Her shirt was wrinkled and she needed a shower, but she was too tired to do anything more than fall into bed in the early hours of the morning when she arrived.

Walking into the house, she looked around. It was empty. Her dad was probably out working on something; but looking at the clock, she realized it was nearing noon. He'd be in for lunch soon. Good, she had a few minutes to come up with a story that was less embarrassing than the truth: she got in her truck to chase a man, and if that weren't pathetic enough, she chickened out and ended up here.

She put on coffee and started rummaging through the cupboards for food. Settling on sandwiches, she went about making lunch for her dad, and breakfast for herself.

The slamming door drew her attention, but she didn't stop. She heard her dad walk in, his boots still on and clumping on the floor. A chair scraped back, and she knew he settled into a seat.

"I wondered when you were going to emerge," he said, and she could hear him unfolding his newspaper.

Tracy turned around, carrying a sandwich over him. "Good to see you too, Dad."

"Got coffee?"

"Just finishing up."

She pulled out two mugs and poured the coffee, serving it to her dad black.

"So, when did you get in?"

"Early this morning."

"Didn't realize you were coming."

"I didn't realize it myself."

"You here long?"

"No idea." She took a bite of her ham and cheese sandwich, waiting for her dad to continue his line of questioning. He remained quiet, though, as he sipped his coffee and ate his lunch, flipping through the small, municipal newspaper.

Once finished, he stood up. "Well, I better get off to work. You sticking around? Or will you suddenly decide to take off and leave again?"

She grimaced. "Sorry, I shouldn't keep doing this to you. It's not fair."

"Can't help but think you're running from something. Problem is, you don't know what you're running toward."

He walked out, leaving Tracy alone in the house.

She busied herself all day, doing the things that her dad usually let slide in his life since becoming a bachelor. Carpets needed vacuuming, floors needed washing, and *everything* needed dusting. Normally, she hated working inside, but today, it was a welcome distraction.

She even made supper, which was *not* something she ever did. It wasn't much, but it was food. When her dad came back in the house for the night, he washed up and sat down at a fully set table.

"Seems you have a bit of your mother in you after all."

"But more of you," she said.

"You ready to tell me what you're running from?"

"Myself," she muttered around a mouthful of food.

Her dad sighed, and she looked up. He seemed sad and pained. "You've become a beautiful and talented woman, Tracy. Please don't run away from who you are."

"I've screwed up plenty, and now I chased away the one guy who could probably have put up with me."

She didn't intend to admit all that to her dad. She always tried to appear strong and capable to him, but she was a mess right now, and the words just tumbled out, accompanied by tears.

"You chased him away, so go get him back," he said matter-of-factly, shoving a bite of potatoes in his mouth.

"It's not that simple."

"It is. You get back in that truck and go get him. It's that simple, and that hard."

"What if he sends me away?"

He set down his fork and looked her in the eyes. "Look, Tracy, I don't like to tell you what to do, but I'm going to do it this time. You get in that truck tomorrow morning and you drive to that boy's home. You tell him how you feel. 'Cause that's what love is. It's taking risks, and giving your heart to someone else for better or for worse. If you can't do that, then you don't truly love him, and maybe you're better off just moving on."

"Dad…"

"I'm serious. Tomorrow, you get in that truck and you either go to him, or you drive to the nearest rodeo and get back on your horse. Those are your options. You aren't hiding here anymore. You're a grown woman and it's time you faced reality."

She closed her eyes, brushing her tears away. She'd never heard her dad sound so vehement about anything. She didn't know what to say in response other than just nodding her consent.

"Love doesn't come around every day, girly. Don't let it slip from your fingers. You're the best roper I know, you can catch anything you set your mind to."

"Except love."

"Yeah, well, most of us have trouble with that."

* * *

Tracy tossed and turned all night and finally, at four a.m., she got up and dressed. She loaded Jack into the trailer and pulled onto Highway 2. She still wasn't sure if she would go to Foremost and her possible future, or to the next rodeo on her list. She figured she'd just drive and see where she ended up.

CHAPTER TWENTY

Carson rolled over and sat up, staring at the alarm clock that still appeared fuzzy to his half-asleep eyes. Reaching forward, he pressed the off button and the room fell into blissful silence. He didn't sleep well last night. Tracy tried calling again around midnight. He still didn't know if he could answer her call, and seriously considered answering the one last night, but only for a second or two before he ignored that one too. He didn't even know what he wanted to hear from her, so how could he hope to have a meaningful conversation?

Getting up, he went about his morning routine a lot slower than usual. He was used to sleeping in the open air of his trailer. Mornings came with the warmth of the sun and the sound of the rodeo grounds awakening.

Here, there was just silence, aside from the sound of his dad puttering about the kitchen. His mom would still be asleep for another hour, and then she'd start making breakfast.

Hobbling out of his bedroom, his crutches clicking on the floor with each step, he joined his dad in the kitchen. He grabbed a mug and poured himself a cup of coffee. Leaning on the counter, he breathed in the steam rising from his cup, and wrapped his hands around the warm mug.

"What's the plan for today?"

"Work," his dad grunted.

"Need help?"

"I always need help."

He frowned, then nodded. "I'm yours to boss around after breakfast."

His dad nodded, popping his toast out of the toaster before it was done, and dropping it on the counter. It was the same routine Carson had watched him do every day of his life, or at least, since he started waking up with his dad. Coffee with two creams and sugars, and two slices of toast, slathered in butter—not margarine; it had to be the real stuff.

Carson liked his coffee black, and food usually waited until his mom got the bacon and eggs going. He sat down at the table across from his dad, though, and drank his coffee in silence. Once his dad finished, he scraped back his chair and deposited his mug in the sink, swiping off the crumbs from his toast onto the floor—a habit that Carson's mom hated, but she couldn't seem to get her husband to stop doing.

"By the way, there's a truck and a rig parked outside."

Carson's head snapped to attention. "What?"

"A white truck; Ford I think. It was there when I got up."

A white Ford truck? It wasn't like there was a lack of trucks like that, but he only knew of one person who would be parked in his driveway with one and hauling a rig. Getting up, he half walked, half swung himself on his crutches to the boot room and opened the door, looking out.

Tracy, what are you doing here?

He shut the door and made his way back into the kitchen, draining the rest of his coffee into the sink. It was cold anyway.

"You going to deal with it?" his dad asked.

"Yep."

"'Cause we aren't running a campground here."

"Maybe you should go tell her that," he grumbled, pulling his boot onto his good foot.

The sun was still rising, washing the yard in a golden light. It would have almost been romantic, if his heart weren't thundering in fear. What would he say to her?

Walking up to the driver's side, he looked in the window. Her seat was reclined and there she was, hat pulled over her face, sleeping. He closed his eyes, letting out a sigh. He was not ready to face her, not only a couple days after everything blew up, but she couldn't just sleep here.

Rapping on the window, he watched her stir, then sit up, her hat falling from her face. She looked exhausted. Her eyes were red and she sported dark circles under them, attesting to the fact that she had very little sleep, and quite possibly was crying—which was hard to believe. The only time he'd seen Tracy cry was when that doctor from Lethbridge treated her like the next notch on his headboard.

She looked at him, offering a half smile, and pushed the door to open it. He stepped aside, letting her out, but crossed his arms. He wasn't about to listen to her nonsense. He just wanted to send her on her way.

"What are you doing here?" he asked, the words coming out a lot harsher than he intended.

"I came to talk."

"The fact that I'm ignoring your calls should have told you that I'm not interested in talking."

"Yeah? Well, you can't ignore me in person," she bit back, her eyes flashing. She looked anything but half asleep now.

"Just say what you have to and be on your way, okay? It's early and this is not how I choose to start my day."

Tracy stood with one hip cocked and her hands planted firmly on either side. She looked ready for a fight. Well, she wasn't going to get one. He was done fighting with her; he just wanted to live his life.

"I'm sorry."

He shook his head, blinking. "I'm sorry?"

"Yes, I'm sorry. I shouldn't have taken the fall out on you. Accidents happen."

"Oh, well, okay."

The words weren't entirely unexpected, but something about Tracy Miller admitting fault stopped him in his tracks. It definitely wasn't an everyday occurrence.

"You drove five hours, through the night, I assume, just to tell me that?"

She looked down, rocking her right foot back and forth in the gravel. "Not exactly."

He sighed. "Can you just spit it out, then? I have a lot to do."

"Iloveyou." Her words tumbled out, all running together and barely understood. Carson's heart started thudding even faster, if that were possible, and sweat caused him to shiver a little.

"You… what?"

She blushed a brilliant shade of red, then looked up at him, meeting his eyes. "Screw it. I don't have to be scared of this. I love you, Carson. Okay? You left and I *cried* over you. I don't cry over guys, ever. But it wasn't even about you leaving. Every time I tried to tell myself to saddle up and move on, all I felt was an empty sadness in my stomach. It made me sick."

Carson stared at her, taking in the words; still not sure he was hearing her right. In his wildest dreams, he never would have imagined her driving up there and telling him she loved him. In fact, he always thought he'd have to be the one to say it, and in one of those instances in their relationship that would either make or break them. But here she stood, saying the words that he was too scared to admit for weeks now.

"Say something."

He opened his mouth, then closed it again. He had no words. Did he tell her that he loved her too? He did, but love didn't magically work everything out.

"Tracy…" he trailed off. He wanted so badly to say the words to her, just as much as her pleading eyes told him she needed to hear them.

"It's okay, I get it. I screwed everything up."

"It's not that. I'm just…" he paused. "I'm scared. If we put our hearts on the line all over again, what comes next? Do we go back on the circuit once I'm better? Make it to pros? And stay spinning our wheels in the same rut we've been in since day one? It can't last that way, Tracy. We have to move forward."

She clenched her jaw, then blew out a deep breath. The loose hair around her face lifted away and floated back. "I'm trying here, Carson. I really am. I think that telling you *I love you* is me putting a little grit under those tires, don't you? All you have to do is give it a push and we'll be moving on."

"I want to, I really do."

"Then kiss me. Do something!"

"I can't. How will I know you're going to put us before your career?"

Her eyes fell, her shoulders drooped, and she kicked the gravel. "I love you, but I love rodeo, too, and I won't walk away from it. But I don't think you want me to. That's why you left. You don't think you can give me what I need, but this is your dream too, and we can share it together."

"You get obsessive."

"And you keep me on track. I can't rope with anyone else. Believe me; I've been around the track when it comes to partners. You're the only one I've been able to work with."

She paused, but he didn't say a word. He wanted her to finish what she had to say without him influencing her.

"I can't promise you that I won't get so focused on our career that I'll let our relationship get stuck. But that's the beauty of this; we are a team. In rodeo, in life… when I start to slide, you bring me back. And when you start feeling a little lost, I pull you back on track. Why can't that work?"

He smiled and walked forward, pulling her into his arms. "Tracy, I love you. I have for a while now, I just wasn't able to say the words."

"Thanks for leaving me hanging," she mumbled into his chest. He smiled, no, he grinned, and she looked up at him with wide eyes. Then she reached up, wrapping her arms around his neck, craning up on her tippy toes. "Kiss me, cowboy."

EPILOGUE

"Our next team hails from Foremost, Alberta," the famous radio voice personality echoed over the loud speaker amidst cheers from the crowd. "Please welcome Carson Walker and Tracy Miller!"

The arena erupted with noise as people cheered and whooped. Never before had Tracy felt so much energy at a rodeo. Then again, it wasn't every day she made it to the Canadian Team Roping Finals. Everyone here was a fan of the sport, and she and Carson managed to make quite a name for themselves this past season.

She swung her leg up and over Jack's back and settled into the saddle. She looked across the chute at Carson. He smiled and tipped his hat at her.

This was it. This was their moment.

Jack danced a little in the chute as the noise washed over them, and she reached down, resting her hand on his neck. "Easy, boy. Save it for the steer."

He immediately calmed, his ears twitching back and forth as he listened. A huff left his nostrils and she could feel his whole body shifting beneath her.

She shortened her reins and evened them out, taking them into her left hand. She caught the sparkle of a ring on her finger and smiled. No one knew yet. Just she and Carson. But they would, once this run was over.

She went through her ritual. Breathe in, breathe out, and looked up again to meet the eyes of her future husband. *Tracy Walker* had a nice ring to it. His eyes seemed to twinkle as he met her gaze and nodded once again, this time to tell her he was ready. She gripped her rope tighter in her right hand and looked out at the sea of people in the stands. One more deep breath, and then...

The chute sprang open and Jack took off. She didn't have to look to see where Danny and Carson were, she *knew* they'd be right where they had to be. Right now, right this second, it was just her rope and that steer. The whirr of the lariat kept time with the frightened animal's mad dash across the arena. Her left hand gripped the reins and Jack's mane, while her right swung the rope wide. Nothing else mattered except for those back legs.

The steer jerked and she knew his head was caught. She watched his muscles bunch, and coil in to explode, waiting for that second when they reached the springing point, and she let her rope fly.

It arched through the air, circling around both back legs of the steer, as she pulled back. Twisting the rope around her saddle horn, Jack braced against the cow.

"That's it folks! A picture perfect run by Carson Walker and Tracy Miller."

Tracy let the rope loosen, allowing the steer to kick free from his confines and Carson ran it to the other end of the arena and the out gate. She followed behind, quietly, waiting for the time to be read aloud.

"Four point nine seconds! They've just set the bar for the competition tonight."

Her face broke into a grin that she couldn't hold back, and she nudged Jack into a canter to join Carson at the out gate.

He'd already dismounted when she rode through, and he reached up, pulling her from Jack as soon as she stopped.

"We did it," he whispered in her ear, holding her in his arms.

"We still have two more days…" she trailed off. "Who cares? You're right, we did it."

She took his face between her hands and kissed him.

"Girly?"

She broke the kiss and looked over Carson's shoulder. "Dad?"

Carson set her down, stepping aside to let her approach her father. "I can't believe you're here!"

"I wouldn't have missed it. You did me proud, girly."

She choked back a tear and ran into her dad's arms. "Thank you," she whispered. "And I've got some more news for you, Dad."

He let her go, holding her at arm's length, his eyes twinkling like he already knew. But she didn't care, she wanted to tell him anyway. "Pretty soon those announcers will be calling us Carson and Tracy *Walker*."

ABOUT THE AUTHOR

Christine Steendam is the award-winning romance author of the Great Canadian Plains Series and the Ocean Series. She also flirts with sci-fi and comic book writing and is a yearly participant in NaNoWriMo.

Christine makes her home in Manitoba, Canada on a sprawling 15 acre ranch with her husband, two young sons, and a brood of animals including Guinness, her beloved chocolate quarter horse; Smokey, her mischievous pony; and her dogs, Beau and Marshall.

www.christinesteendam.com
kcsteendam@gmail.com

Other books by Christine Steendam

The Ocean Series
Owned by the Ocean
Heart Like an Ocean
Betrayed by the Ocean

The Great Canadian Plains Series
Unforgiving Plains
Ropes & Reins

Other Fiction
Shadows of the Unseen